To: Current Occupant

Zerry Greenwood

Zerry Greenwood

Chapter One

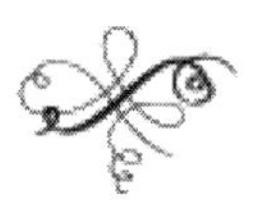

In 1871, Lavina Randall's uncle, Rufus Bullock, was the most hated Republican in Georgia. At the end of the civil war, Rufus entered politics and won his run for Governor against a former Confederate general, John B. Gordon. What a beautiful restart for the south after the war, or so one would think.

However, abolitionists Bullock's stand on black equality, which included blacks holding office and one man, one vote, flew in the face of his adversary. As head of the Ku Klux Klan, John Gordon, and his men in sheets all but tarred and feathered Governor Bullock before they ran him out of town.

Lavina Randall was a Bullock on her mother's side and could stay in Georgia with a certain amount of anonymity. But Uncle Rufus was the one constant in her life, and she was proud to call him kin.

Raised believing that color played no part in what made a man good or evil, Lavina had a sudden urge to be as far away from Atlanta as one could be. To stay in a place where people were so narrow-minded lost its appeal. *They have drawn a line in the sand for the Bullock Family, and this southern bell plans on being on the right side of it.*

The last few months had been a whirlwind of goodbyes to family as they fled Georgia for better prospects. *Now is the time to take a leap. Might as well make it a big one.*

Lavina packed everything she thought she might have a use for into the biggest trunk she could find. It held a service of China, silver flatware, and tea set. Quilts, sheets, and a set of towels for both the bath and kitchen. A small library, journals, ink, and stationery with the governor's seal. Not that Lavina ever entered the gubernatorial home, but her uncle brought stationery whenever he visited.

Family photos in gilded frames were inside, as well as her most beloved art box. Toiletries and every item of clothing she owned, from hats to boots, found a new home. Last but not least, she packed her mother's jewelry and closed the lid. *Not even room left for a handkerchief.*

She examined her handbag one last time. It held her tickets, the derringer her uncle referred to as the man-stopper, the letters from Ted, and a tintype of her parents. Lavina had no actual memories of her parents, just a sense of love. A commodity her family was in short supply of and which her money could not buy. *Mama, I feel your hand in this affair. I do not fear my future.* Lavina tucked two hundred dollars in her corset and called for a porter.

At five years old, Lavina's parents died, and she spent her childhood passed from one of her mother's relatives to the next. They never kept her in one home for longer than two years. Her relatives were more than happy to take her money, but once they realized it came with her attached, they sent her to the next relative. Uncle Rufus was ten years her senior and more of a cousin, but he checked in on her whenever he was in town. Most of her other relatives made themselves mighty scarce after she left their homes.

At eighteen, she settled in a suite of rooms at the Whitehall Inn on the outskirts of Atlanta. The last two years Lavina spent on its veranda painting the restoration after Sherman's march to the sea and sipping tea with vain gold diggers, young and old. *What a narrow existence I live.* Lavina never indulged in dreams or aspirations. *Happiness either happens or it does not.* This had been her philosophy for years. *Not anymore. I will seek to ensure my happiness from this day forward.*

She followed her trunk and the porter through the hall into the lobby and held her head high. *Nothing in my decision is cause for shame. A good man awaits me, and these people can kiss my lily-white arse.*

Lavina did not thank the hotel's self-righteous staff, who spent the last two months snubbing her. The hotel's lackeys had been more than willing to cater to her every whim these last two years. But alas, her large tips no longer squelched their anger towards her uncle's call for equal economic opportunities and the education of the freedmen.

I will shake the sand of Atlanta, Georgia from my shoes and sink them into the welcoming soil of Atlanta, Idaho.

Her aunt and uncle moved to New York months earlier, so there was no one at the train station to cry, kiss her goodbye, or wish her farewell. However, this was not the first time she departed without the customary emotional farewell to family and friends. Most times family was too busy making sure her belongings were on board, for fear she might need to return for something or another. Her honest opinions were not always welcome on the Bullock side of the family.

Once Georgia was out of view, Lavina walked out the back entrance of the train and let the breeze blow away the ignorance of the suffocating South. *I wonder how far west one needs to go to get out of its boorish oppression.* She leaned over the railing and reread Ted's letters and advertisement.

The advertisement had drawn her into an idea that might have otherwise been repugnant. Number twenty-two's ad read; The silver and gold of the Idaho mountains called me by name. But women it did not draw the same. So here I sit with home and riches alongside other two-legged creatures wearing britches. I miss the touch of a woman's soft skin and wish to smell something other than sweaty men. If you are in search of a man who is steady and true, send your letters to number twenty-two.

Someone had left a copy of The Matrimonial News in the hotel lobby, and she perused it for entertainment. The advertisement caused her to laugh aloud the first time she read it. Later, as she unlocked her door to suite number twenty-two, she found humor in the coincidence. However, the next morning when her breakfast cost twenty-two cents and the hansom cab she took to visit her aunt was number twenty-two, Lavina saw it as a sign from the universe.

After having bid her aunt and uncle goodbye, she wrote her first letter to number twenty-two and sent it to the newspaper. To appear playful, Lavina wrote back in iambic pentameters.

Number Twenty-two,

The atmosphere of the post-war South is thick.

And my spirit yearns as if it were homesick.

That all men will treat each other equally is debatable.

And the atmosphere here has grown quite unpalatable.

I have aspirations the South can no longer quench.

From arduous work and compromise, I do not flinch.

A future far from here is my only desire.

But fair warning, I can be a spitfire.

Lavina Randall

Suite 22, Whitehall Inn.

Atlanta, Georgia

Number twenty-two was from a town by the name of Atlanta as well, and this added to her notion of it being fortuitous.

Ted Bartlett's advertisement and letters were impressive. His home was at the base of Greylock Mountain, at the foot of the Sawtooth Mountain range in a meadow, with green pastures and luxurious waterways. The middle fork of the Boise River ran through it, and a thermal waterfall of indescribable splendor was on the edge. The miners named the unique feature Chattanooga Hot Springs. *My goodness. It sounds heavenly.*

Ted talked of an area on his land where she could put in a garden. *For a woman who never even picked her own flowers, this will prove interesting.* He talked of purchasing a milk cow and chickens for her. *Oh goodness, what a pampered princess I have been. I will need to purchase work gloves and boots.*

Ted's ore mine was a half day's walk north and showed excellent color, according to his letter. His house was a small two-story home, but once he had his mine operational, he intended to let her design the house of her dreams. *What is the house of my dreams? I have lived in beautiful houses and luxurious hotels. A home, a proper home, with love and laughter, is my only desire.*

His property was a good stretch of the legs, east of town. Secluded enough to allow them a private life away from the other miners, but not so far that she will be lonely. *Surrounded by people my entire life, I have found nothing but loneliness. I only hope to have one person to keep me company.*

Ted filled his first letter with descriptions of himself, his mine, his house, and the land. He included a list of his expectations of the woman he might wish to marry. Ted talked of his hope of her having a deep faith, a desire for children, and a wish for tenderness. He did not mention looks or list appearances as important to him.

Lavina thought this spoke well of his character. Not that she needs to worry over her looks. Everyone acclaimed her mother as a Nordic beauty. Lavina inherited her mother's blond hair with auburn streaks and a slight curl. Her small nose, long lashes, and light-blue eyes were her mother's as well. At five feet ten inches, Lavina was average weight, with a nice build.

His second letter talked of improvements and equipment he needed to run his mining operation and build his new home. He never asked concerning a dowry or if she possessed money, and again this impressed Lavina. Money was not an issue either. When her parents died, they left her with a small fortune from her father's side of the family.

Ted's third letter was a suggestion for her to visit and if everything was to her liking, marriage. She decided the land and opportunity were to her liking, and his character and humor appeared pleasing. Lavina possessed talent, humor, and strength. These were the traits she hoped for in a life partner. *I think we will make an excellent match.*

As the train pulled into a station somewhere in Kansas, Lavina headed to the bunk assigned her. The farther north the train traveled, Lavina noticed two things. One, the heat was no longer an issue. She needed to pull out a jacket and quilt to stay warm. The second, more surprising aspect of her trip was how the Rocky Mountains gave her a sense of homecoming.

As Lavina hiked in the dark to the tiny cabin, she felt her anger boil to the top. The hem of her dress and slippers were filthy and her feet ached from stepping on rocks she could not see. *He best be in their dying.*

From the light of a window, she spotted Ted's head bent over a book. *Reading! I will kill him.* She kicked open the door and glared as he jumped to his feet. He towered over her and his dark good looks were intimidating. *Stand your ground, say your piece.*

"Well, if this isn't a fine how do you do," she screamed. "Four days on a train. Three days in an overcrowded stagecoach with smelly miners who did not understand a word I said," she announced in her thick southern drawl. "I waited for a half-hour before I gave up and started walking." Lavina's body vibrated with anger. "I left my trunk, with everything I own in the world, on the side of the road."

She saw the giant open his mouth to speak. "Shut up," she screamed again. "You need to hook up a buckboard and fetch my trunk before it rains, or snows, or I don't know, a bear tears it apart." Her mouth dropped open as she took in her surroundings.

She stood in a large room. One end had rough lumber counters, a metal tub, and a wood cookstove. In front of her were a small table and four kitchen chairs. The other end of the room held a small desk and two padded rockers on either side of what she could only describe as a fire pit. Behind the mountain of a man was a single door, and beside him was a ladder that led to a loft.

"Oh no! No, no. Let me make this clear, my idea of a two-story house is not a loft with a ladder." Lavina pushed past him to open the door behind him. "I'm not crawling up that death trap. I will take this room." She watched as he lit another lantern and moved towards the door. "I am going to bed. I only pray that my anger does not haunt my dreams."

She walked into the dark bedroom, then came out and snatched the lantern off the table. "I have a gun. If you step one foot in this room tonight, I will use it." She slammed the door on his shocked expression.

It was late and the quiet giant did not bother to hook his team up to the wagon. He made the short walk to the stage stop and back on foot. It was an hour before he carried in the angry woman's large, cumbersome trunk.

With practiced stealth, he climbed the ladder into the loft. Tilly lay at the edge of the bed, one olive-skinned arm and a leg flung over the side. Cliff smiled at the tender picture she made. He rolled the dark-haired beauty to the center and crawled in beside her. Milly, her twin who slept against the wall, leaned on her elbow and gave him a crooked smile. "Who was that woman yelling at you?"

"I have no idea. I guess we will find out in the morning." He gave her a soft kiss goodnight. "I love you."

"I love you too, Pa."

Cliff Walters pulled his girls to him. "Sweet dreams, baby girl," he whispered, then drifted into a *haunted* dream.

Chapter Two

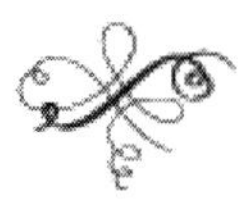

As Cliff put on his shirt, Tilly and Milly giggled and crawled out of bed. "Sh," he said and pulled on his boots. "There is a rattlesnake sleeping in my bed." He kissed the girls on their heads and mussed their hair. "Best not poke her this morning."

In silence, they crawled down the ladder in single file. "I will put on coffee," he whispered. "You both go out and check if the hens have started to lay again." It had been three weeks since they moved to Idaho and the stress of the trip from Montana caused the hens to off lay. As the girls headed out the door, Cliff heard movement from his bedroom. *This should be an interesting morning.* He pulled out a pair of tin coffee mugs and awaited the stranger's exit from his bedroom.

The woman entered as the coffee came to a boil, and Cliff greeted her with a bob of his head. "Good morning. Coffee?" Cliff stood six feet, five inches, and had dark olive skin. His nose was evidence of a hard life and made two small turns. Dark, tight curls covered his head and face while his black eyes held a twinkle this morning.

She cleared her throat and patted down her dress. "Yes, please." Her voice was shaky as she sat across from Cliff while he poured them coffee. "It's a little late for good first impressions," she said, then took a sip of coffee. "So, shall we make a fresh start of it instead?"

"Sounds good to me." Cliff reached out a hand to introduce himself when Milly and Tilly busted through the door. His girls were gorgeous, identical twins. At four feet and five inches, they were tall for eight years of age. Their skin tone was a light olive color, while their eyes were dark green and the only resemblance to their mother. All other attributes were their fathers, including their dark hair and tight curls.

"Pa, Pa, they are back to laying," Tilly announced.

Milly opened her apron on the table to reveal six brown eggs. "We found half a dozen."

Cliff did not look at the eggs. He enjoyed the shock that covered the stranger's face as if someone had drawn closed a set of heavy drapes. A slow tug, tug, tug before they swept together in a thwap.

"Pa? Are you, their father?" Her jaw hung open as she stared first at the girls, then back at him.

He held back a chuckle as he watched her blink in rapid succession, then stood and walked behind his girls. "Yes, this is Milly." He mussed the child's hair, then said, "And this is Tilly." He did the same to the second child and watched as the woman gawked at the three of them.

A sharp shake of her head brought a frenzied look in her eye as she pulled letters from a purse that hung on her wrist. She flipped through them as she shook her head. "Why did you not mention this?" The final word came out in a high-pitched squeal.

Cliff chuckled, then returned to his seat and sipped his coffee. "When might I have mentioned it?" His tone was calculative and calm.

The stranger tossed her mail on the table and spoke with a not-so-practiced patience as he. "In your letters." Her eyes bugged at the scattered parchment. "I think that was a rather important detail you left out."

Cliff squinted at the scattered mail as a slight grin came to his lips and the twinkle came back into his eye. "Are you looking for Ted?" He snapped his fingers at the girls. "Tilly, hand me that paper." Tilly found it on the desk and delivered it to her father, who scanned the paper in search of the last name. "That's right. Are you looking for Ted Bartlett?"

He watched as the woman flushed red while realization filled her face. "Oh goodness. I am so sorry." She reached out and touched Cliff's forearm. "I must have appeared stark raving mad last night."

Cliff pursed his lips and shrugged. "Your words, not mine."

"Yeah, Pa never said you was crazy, he said you was a rattlesnake." Cliff glared Tilly into silence.

"I'd say he made a fair assessment, considering my behavior last night." Lavina's smile offered sympathy to the now shamefaced child. "I must have taken a wrong turn in the dark, darling."

Milly leaned against her father's arm and pulled the bill of sale out of his hand. "No ma'am, you're in the right place. Pa bought this ranch from Mister Bartlett for a steal, last month."

Cliff swallowed his laughter as the woman's eyes widened. "Last month?" she sputtered.

Tilly chose that moment to add coals to the fire. "That's right. Mister Bartlett was in a big rush to get out of here and go east somewhere."

Cliff watched as the stranger's shoulders bobbed before her nervous giggles began. "Ha hah, oh. Oh, no." She rubbed the brim of her nose as confusion covered his girl's faces. "Dear me, ha hah. Oh, goodness." The woman placed her head on the table while the girls drew closer to Cliff. "Bless my soul. I am an idiot." She bounced her head on the wooden surface and moaned.

Cliff held his finger to his lips and pulled the girls back as they moved to comfort her.

Lavina lifted her head and gave them a creepy, awkward grin. "Well." She stood and patted down her dress before she opened the door. "If you will excuse me, I think I'll look around." She then gave a soft snort and walked out. "For a hole or a well, I can throw myself into."

When she was out of view, the twins stared at their father wide-eyed.

"What was that all about?" Milly asked.

Tilly took a more concerned stance. "Is she serious?"

He pulled a newspaper clipping from under her letters on the table and read. "Well, that can't feel good."

Milly and Tilly peered over his shoulder. "What does it say?"

Cliff stood and tucked the advertisement back under the pile of letters before he announced, "She is a Mail-order bride." He opened the door and stepped out as he left orders for the twins. "You girls fry up potatoes and eggs. I will fetch her back."

Lavina admired the craggy mountain peaks while she pulled apart the heads of wild grain. The cautious footsteps of the good-looking giant interrupted her silent beratement of her foolish decisions.

"Are you better now?" He cocked his head to look in her face.

She gave him a shrug. "I had a pleasant train ride, and I saw some magnificent country. It wasn't a total loss."

"What will you do now? Go back home?"

Tears filled her eyes, and her chin quivered. "There is no going home to Georgia and no one to go home to." She wiped her cheeks and said, "I am not sure just what I will do now."

He pulled her shoulders back in a reassuring gesture and aimed her toward the house. "You can't think or make good decisions on an empty stomach. My girls will have breakfast ready by now."

Lavina followed the giant, then walked through the door he held open.

Milly smiled as they entered and placed two more plates on the table. "Breakfast is served."

Lavina laid a hand on the girl's shoulder and squeezed. "Bless your heart," she whispered through her grief.

Tilly held up the coffee pot to the stranger and asked, "Would you like more coffee?"

Lavina smiled at the child as warmth reentered her heart. "Thank you, darling. I would love a refill."

When everyone sat at the table, Lavina picked up her fork and began to eat. The others held hands and reached out to her. She blushed and placed her fork back on her plate. When they bowed their heads, she winked and smiled at the twins while their father prayed in his deep timbre. When Cliff finished, Lavina spoke with newfound resolve. "I guess if we are going to break bread together, we should get more acquainted with one another. My name is Lavina Randall, and I am from Atlanta, Georgia."

"That is a pretty name." One girl remarked, but Lavina was unsure which.

"Thank you, and what is your name again?"

The girls looked at each other and giggled. "I am Tilly, and she is Milly."

Lavina leaned across the table and scrutinized the girl's features. "Tilly has a tiny scar in her brow." She licked her thumb and traced the child's sparse eyebrow. "I'll show you how to fill that in when you get older." She squinted at the other child and said, "And Milly has a mole near her ear. I'll show you how to pluck the hair out of it, so they don't burn you as a witch by mistake."

Both girls touched their faces. "You're smart," they said in unison.

Lavina's eyes rolled as she mocked herself. "Current circumstances would prove otherwise." The good-looking giant sat mute, and Lavina nodded his way. "And what do they call your daddy?"

The girls giggled again, and Milly replied, "Cliff."

Lavina sat back and sipped her coffee while her eyes scanned every inch of the man. "That suits him. He is a mountain, isn't he?"

Cliff looked up from his plate and smiled. "My name is Cliff Walters," he said to Lavina, then addressed the twins. "Girls go catch Maggie; she needs to be milked." When the girls ran out the door, he stood and placed the dishes in a tub, which served as a kitchen sink. "Some of my family lives in Atlanta, Georgia as well."

Lavina walked to the stove and filled her cup once more. "I can imagine that was difficult on your mother." She leaned against the counter and sipped her coffee. "And you, for that matter. I do not suppose in those days a mixed child was at all welcome in Atlanta."

"No, I don't suppose. That is why when my grandmother found out her daughter was pregnant with a black man's child; she shipped her west to Montana. My mother raised me by herself on a small farm her father purchased during the war. I have never been to Georgia and have no desire to."

"I don't suppose you ever heard of my uncle, Rufus Bullock?"

"The abolitionist governor? That the KKK ran out of town?"

Lavina stepped back and gave him a dubious glance. "Now, how did you come to acquire that bit of information?"

"My father's family informed me. They still live in Atlanta. The governor's expulsion from Georgia was a great disappointment to them."

"I did not think of that. Maybe someday Georgia will be more accepting of a progressive abolitionist and my uncle can move back. But for now, he and his family are not welcome. So, you see, I truly am homeless at the moment." Lavina put her now empty cup into the tub. "How did you come to be in Atlanta, Idaho, raising two children alone?"

"After I married my wife, I brought her back to help with my mother's farm in Montana. She died giving birth to our girls."

"Glory be." Lavina touched his arm. "I am deeply sorry for your loss. But your girls seem happy so you must be getting along, just the three of you."

"The girls and I have done fine." He put on a jacket and snapped up the collar. "Last year my mother took ill and died two months ago. That is when I wrote to my father's family and my grandmother."

"You know your father, then?" she asked with a little too much surprise, then gathered her letters and placed them back in her clutch to avoid Cliff's scowl.

"No, I never met him, and now I never will. He died years ago according to his sister."

"Bless your heart, you have had quite the run of bad luck, with your many losses."

"Loss or gain. Who can tell? We never heard from my father but once, and that was a note to my mother, to say his family agreed with her mother. That they should go on with their lives as if nothing happened."

"Of course." Lavina let out a snort of disgust. "Nothing happened to him. He was not pregnant and alone, carrying a mixed child in a world full of hatred." Lavina placed a hand over her mouth and stammered, "I am sorry, I had no right."

"What did you say that was not true?" Cliff shrugged and continued. "My father's sister wrote at length concerning her regret that we never met. Pretty words after the fact, and considering the expulsion of your uncle, I doubt his family would be any more thrilled to claim me now."

Lavina twisted her purse. "What did your grandmother have to say?"

Cliff shook his head and snorted. "She stayed true to her colors. I believe her exact words were, get your black ass off my property so I can sell it and recoup my losses."

Lavina's head snapped up. "Lordy. I am without words. Now there is some real southern hospitality for you."

"Yes, I agree. But we granted her that wish, and now here we are, in Atlanta." Cliff put on his hat and gave her a broad smile.

Glory be. A girl could trip in those dimples.

"Pa, we caught Maggie." Lavina jumped as the girls called from outside the door. Cliff picked up a pail and walked out to milk the cow, which left her alone with her thoughts.

What an ignorant world in which we live. Lavina followed him out and watched the tender picture of the girls petting the cow while their father stroked their heads. "Thank you, baby girls. I can take her from here."

As he took the rope from Tilly, Lavina asked, "If you have this, Mister Walters, do you mind if the girls walk to town with me?"

Milly and Tilly squealed while they tugged his shirt sleeves and pleaded, "Please, Pa, can we go?"

Cliff raised a dubious brow. "Town?"

"Yes, I am not sure what I want to do just yet, but I can't keep sleeping in your bed. I will ask around for a place to rent. Maybe they have a hotel or even a boarding house."

Cliff snorted. "We have only been to town once. Not much to see. You can take the girls."

Lavina clapped. "Come, girls, let us do the dishes and sweep the floor first. While we are in town, I will buy the makings for a pie." She smiled at Cliff and laced her words with sugar-coated congeniality. "What is your favorite pie, Mister Walters?"

"Strawberry rhubarb." He strolled away with the cow. "Good luck with that, too."

Lavina smoothed her dress, then shooed the girls in the door ahead of her. "Mister Walters, never underestimate the determination of a desperate woman."

It took less than five minutes for them to clean the room when Lavina clapped again. "Very nice ladies, now run upstairs and change, quick-like."

The girls looked at one another, then back to Lavina. "Change what?" Tilly asked.

"Well silly, out of your grungy work clothes and into something pretty."

"We only have one other dress and it's for church." Milly scoffed.

"That's no never mind." Lavina fanned the air with one nervous hand. "You can just slip on your pinafores."

Tilly scrunched her little face. "What's a pinafore?"

Oh, Lavina child, learn to keep your mouth shut. Heat rose in her cheeks as she tried to cover her faux pas. "Why it's an apron of sorts, it covers your whole dress and has frills." She fluffed up her shoulder pads as an indication of how a pinafore might look. "Oh, never mind, just ditch those aprons you have on. What you're wearing is fine." She turned away to gather her composure.

As the girls pulled off their aprons, Milly whispered to Tilly, "I guess we are just supposed to forget she called them grungy work clothes."

Lavina spun and examined the outspoken child. "My, my, Milly. Your tongue is as sharp as a viper's. I see I am going to have to make quite an effort to keep on your good side."

CHAPTER THREE

As they hiked down the road to Atlanta, the girls explained to Lavina they had only seen the town once and it was at night. "Lovely, I enjoy sharing new experiences with new friends. Now when we are old and think of Atlanta, we will always think of each other and this trip to town. We will have to make it an excellent memory."

Tilly entwined her fingers in Lavina's gloved hand. "How will we do that?"

They turned off the road towards town when Lavina spotted a small pond with a flock of Canadian geese. "Some things you make happen, and others are fortuitous." She pointed to the waterfowl.

The girls watched in awe as the goslings swam in lines behind their mothers. "Why do they do that, you think?" Tilly asked.

"They do that to resist drag; it makes swimming easier for the babies." When Lavina continued to walk, Milly and Tilly lined out behind her. "Girls, I am not a goose."

The girls ran up beside her, and Milly whispered to Tilly. "With that bump on her hind end, she walks like one."

"I heard that, and I will remember you said it." Lavina cut her eyes down on the child. "And it is not a bump, it is a bustle, and the height of ladies' fashion." Both girls giggled.

"Why do women want their bottoms to look so big," Tilly asked.

Lavina's feet froze as her jaw dropped. "Goodness, how rude. It is not to make my bottom look big. It is there to keep my skirt from dragging in the dirt."

"Why don't you just wear a straight skirt? Then it would not drag the ground and you could do stuff," Tilly said.

Lavina raised her brow. "Do stuff? What stuff?"

"Walk without looking like a goose," Milly said before bursting into laughter.

Lavina tossed her nose in the air and proceeded forward. "Hush your mouth," she teased, then stuck her tongue at them. "Hum. If it is all the same to you, I think I will block out this memory."

Once Atlanta came into view, Lavina lost hope of finding accommodations. *Does not look very promising.* Situated in a draw between two mountains and built precariously on hillsides were mines and small homes. The town was a single street with a few shops and only single-floor buildings. Further along, Lavina spotted an extensive building that appeared to possess possibilities. She and the girls stepped into The Hub to discover it was a diner, bar, and dance hall all in one open space.

"Can I help you, ladies?" The gentleman behind the bar asked as he scanned Lavina from head to toe in a manner that made her flinch.

She pushed the girls behind her. "No. I was hoping this establishment was a hotel or boarding house."

"In Atlanta?" he snorted. The man had a long handlebar mustache with disheveled hair and a lustful look in his eye, which unnerved Lavina.

"I take it, there is no such thing here," she said while she backed the girls toward the door.

"No, ma'am." He spat towards a copper pot on the floor and missed.

Lavina glanced at him and grimaced. "Are there any rentals you know of?"

The man wiped the bar with a cloth, then used it to wipe the spittle from his mustache before he winked at Lavina as she held back the urge to vomit. "No, but a pretty, little miss like you should have no trouble finding a welcoming bed."

Oh no. He did not just say that in front of these babies. Lavina walked backward and pushed the girls out the door. When they reached the steps, she bent and whispered, "Stay here, and don't talk to anyone. I will be right back."

As she made her slow saunter up to the barkeeper, she calmed her anger as he licked his lips. "You need to learn manners," she said in a tone. A tone which, had he known her better, might have sealed his lips. But he did not know Miss Lavina Randall and chose to speak again.

"Why don't you come back here and teach me some." He then laughed until his chewing tobacco choked him.

While he gagged and coughed, Lavina smoothed her dress. "If I were not wearing my best dress, I would crawl over this bar." She pulled a silver folding knife from her purse and snapped out the blade before she continued. "And make you into a gelding." She shot out her hand to stick the knife into the bar inches from his elbow, then watched with satisfaction as the color drained from his face. "Now, where would I find a grocer?"

The bartender pointed one shaky finger as he sputtered, "Just up the road, ma'am. You can't miss it."

"Thank you." She pulled her knife from the wooden bar. "Now that is information I can use." She pocketed her knife and flounced out the door where the girls stood dumbfounded. She grabbed them by the hand and strolled up the street without a look backward.

Milly leaned behind her bustle and whispered to Tilly. "She sure told him."

Lavina tugged them forward. "Girls, you need to stop that, ladies do not whisper."

"You whispered to us," Tilly said as she gave her an accusing glare.

"Yes, but I was talking to you, not about you." She stopped and tilted her head at them. "Do you understand the difference?"

"Yes." Milly stuck out her lower lip and bowed her head. "Sorry."

Lavina placed her hands on her hips and furrowed her brow. *Her tone is all sass and no sorry.* She brushed it off and continued up the street. "No harm, no foul. But you are right, I will haunt his dreams tonight." As she pushed forward to the market, Lavina gave them a proper lesson in manners. "*Ladies,* wait until they are safe in their own homes, where they talk in delicate tones about others."

Tilly giggled, then asked, "Why did that man talk to you that way?"

Lavina rolled her eyes. "Oh, there are men who think that manner of talk makes a woman all flittery."

"Does it?" Milly asked.

"Me? No. It makes me want to snatch him bald."

The twins giggled and Milly said, "I like the way you talk."

"Do you like the words or the southern accent?"

"Both, but mostly the way you say the words. Slow like." She mimicked Lavina as best she could.

Lavina smiled to herself. *And I was forever being told to talk slower.* She recalled one ignorant teacher's reprimand, 'You talk just like a Jew.' Lavina spent the rest of that school day in the hallway writing, *I will not call Miss Bell ignorant white trash,* five hundred times.

When they arrived at the mercantile, Lavina held the door and ushered the girls inside. Two men stood at the counter. One stood behind and wore a white apron and sleeve guards. He was fairly short and wiry, with a full beard and bald head. The other leaned against the counter and held a newspaper. He was over six feet with a scarred left cheek and blond hair.

Basic food supplies, sundries, and what Lavina guessed was mining equipment filled the store. “Good morning, gentlemen.”

They eyed her and the girls. “Good morning. How can I help you?” asked the man from behind the counter.

Lavina moved toward them with little hope and said, “I was hoping to find a place to rent.”

Both men laughed, and the one who held the paper spoke first. “Not around here. As fast as one miner gives up, three more come to replace him.”

“My goodness.” She sighed. “Well then, I will take a pound of white sugar, five pounds of flour, and a half-pound of brown sugar.” She scanned the room with disappointment. “Do you have rhubarb and strawberries?”

“I have rhubarb in the backyard but that is a no on the strawberries.” His voice revealed his reluctance to do any gardening today.

“How much will you charge me for two stalks?” Lavina asked in her most congenial voice.

“A penny.” There was a thick, sluggish quality to his tone. “Shall I go get it for you?”

Lavina leaned against the counter and batted her lashes. “If you would doll, I would be ever so grateful.” He jumped up and ran out the back of the store and Lavina gave the giggling Milly a wink.

Tilly tugged her sleeve. “Miss Lavina, what will you do for strawberries?”

“If I had put on lip rouge this morning, I imagine I could get him to grow them for me.” She moved around the counter and picked out a jar of strawberry preserves. “However, we do not have that kind of time, so I will improvise.”

“Miss Lavina?” The man at the counter folded his newspaper and raised a brow. “Lavina Randall?”

She set the jar of preserves on the counter and gave him a dubious glance. “Do I know you?”

"No, but I know of you."

Oh goodness, what has he read?

"Ted Bartlett came in every day for three weeks looking for a letter from you." He tapped her arm with his paper.

She relieved him of it and rolled it tight. "Did he now?" She popped his arm with a subtle warning to walk lightly on the subject.

"Yes, ma'am." He retrieved his paper from her grip with great caution. "I run the post office and the saloon down the way. Your letter came two days after he left town."

Relief rushed in on Lavina's thoughts. "Are you telling me he never received my last letter?"

"No, ma'am. I have it in my dead letterbox," he said as he flattened out his paper with an extreme amount of care. "Would you like it back?"

"Yes, please." There was a lilt to her voice now. When the postmaster left to retrieve her letter, Lavina announced to the girls, "Do you comprehend what this means?"

"No," they answered in unison.

Lavina kissed the tops of their heads. "It means he did not run away from me." She raised her brows in rapid succession. "He did not know I was coming." She then placed her hands on her heart and spoke to the ceiling. "Bless my soul. This leaves hope."

Tilly squinched her little face. "Hope?

Lavina straightened and patted her dress. "Yes. Hope! Hope is what ladies hold on to in desperate times. And I'm going to cling to it like a thirty-year-old spinster."

The proprietor came in with eight fresh stalks of rhubarb in a basket and sat it on the counter. Lavina searched through and found two of the ripest. "Thank you, Sir. That will be everything for now. Oh, wait." She gave him a flirtatious wink, then opened a jar on the counter and pulled out three peppermint sticks. "Add these." She handed the girls one each and stuck the other in her mouth. "Can you put the supplies in a gunny sack?" she said as she slid the peppermint stick in and out on her tongue. "We are on foot today."

The proprietor stopped packing them in the crate and searched behind the counter for a sack as the bell on the front door jingled. "Here is your letter." Lavina spun and grabbed it from the postmaster's outreached hand. "Seems it was misrouted to Atlanta, Indiana. Which is too bad. Ted was desperate to hear from you."

"Bless your heart." Lavina stuck it in her pocket and gave him a small curtsy.

The postmaster reached out to touch her arm and said, "The last time he was in he remarked how once he had money and an active mine, he intended to concentrate on his love life."

Lavina brushed away his sympathetic hand and turned to pay the grocer. "Men are so silly. The South is littered with wealthy men. I came west to find adventure, not riches."

The proprietor had bagged her groceries in three small flour sacks and handed one to each of them. "Thank you, very kind." Lavina then gave him an exaggerated smile and a deep curtsy. "Come, ladies."

On the stoop, Milly asked, "Why were you acting so funny to that man?"

Lavina giggled. "There is a saying that goes never bite the hand that feeds you?"

"He is a grocer. I don't think they can bite people," Tilly interrupted.

Lavina gave her a blank stare. "What?" She fanned the air. "Oh, never mind that. I say, a little flirting with the grocer gets you the freshest cuts of meat."

The girls rolled their eyes and continued walking. When they were safely out of town and on the road home, Lavina addressed them again. "Alright darlings, you're going to need to help me with your daddy."

Milly and Tilly looked at each other and then cut their eyes back at her. "How?" asked Tilly.

"I need you to talk me up. Help your daddy understand I could be an asset to y'all. I can teach you girls to cook and sew and... Are you in school?"

"No."

Lavina clapped. "See there. I can teach y'all to read and write and your numbers."

"Will you do all of that?" Suspicion laced Milly's voice.

Lavina placed her hand on her heart. "I swear. I will do all those things and more. But listen, you cannot just run home and start telling him all this at once." She squatted and looked the girls in the face. "You have to be sly with the method you choose to tell him. Do you comprehend how to be sly?"

The girls eyed each other again. Tilly shook her head while Milly answered in the thickest Southern accent she could muster. "She is the honest twin, but my middle name is Sly."

Lavina hugged the girls to her. "Oh, you are just too delicious. I could eat you up. Someone get me a spoon."

Once they were in view of the homestead, Lavina spotted Cliff at the far end of the field where he was building fence. She gave Milly's bottom a pop to urge her. "Run along now, Milly Sly, and help your daddy." She winked, then grasped Tilly's hand and headed to the cabin. "Your sister and I will start dinner and bake your daddy his favorite pie."

Chapter Four

Cliff watched Milly cross the field to join him and smiled. "How was your trip to town?"

"Exciting, a man made a rude comment to Lavina, and she set him in his place. You would have liked it, Pa."

"Where is your sister?"

"Lavina is teaching her how to bake."

Cliff straightened and rubbed his lower back. "You did not want to learn?"

Milly gave him a sly smile. "Oh, I want to learn, but Lavina said we need to all share the work and sent me to help you."

I recognize that smile. What are you cooking up, baby girl? Cliff cut his eyes at her. "Hum, I guess then you can carry my tools." He walked to the next fencepost and pulled the wire tight. "Grab a staple and hammer it in."

Milly reached into the bucket and pulled out a staple then said, "We did not see a school in town."

Cliff's arm started to cramp. It took her a ridiculous amount of effort to hammer the staple in tight. "School? Were you thinking of going to school?" He pulled the second wire tight.

"Tilly and I are almost nine years old, and we do not know our letters or numbers. I bet Lavina knew her letters when she was six." She hammered in another staple.

I smell a plot. Cliff tightened the bottom wire before he replied. "She lived in a big city with lots of schools. I will see if we can find you girls an early reader in town." He watched as her face fell. *What are you scheming baby girl?*

They walked to the next post, and he waited for her to give away her plan. "I like the way she talks," Milly spoke in a thick drawl. "Slow, like she is singing."

Cliff pulled the wire tight and smiled at her change of subject. "Yes, your grandmother had a southern drawl. When I was a child, it slowly fell away."

"I did not think that could happen."

"If you're exposed to different people long enough, your accent changes."

"Maybe I will get one. *Y'all.*"

"I said if you are exposed to it long enough. Miss Randall will not be here long enough for that." Cliff could see Milly wanted to say more, but she showed great restraint. They finished ten posts before she spoke again.

"You should have seen the face of that man when Lavina said she would make him a gelding."

Cliff snorted. "What? Why would she say such a thing?"

Milly bit her lower lip. "I ah... I guess because he was being a pig."

Cliff bent, grabbed the bottom wire, and squinted into her face. "What are you not telling me?"

Milly's words flooded out in a panic. "Lavina did not know it was a bar when we walked in, Pa. I promise."

Cliff chuckled. "A bar?"

"Yes, and the man behind it said something rude to Lavina. She took us outside, then went back and said if she weren't in her best dress, she would make him a gelding."

Cliff fell back on his bottom and burst into laughter. "Poor man, he did not see that coming, I am sure." When he stood, his shirt sleeve caught on a barb and ripped. "Dang, this was my best work shirt."

Milly reached out and touched his arm. "Lavina said she would teach us to sew. This could be my first project."

"Hum. She is going to teach you to bake and sew all before she leaves tonight?"

Milly's eyes widened, and her jaw dropped open. "Well, well, she ah... she might not leave tonight."

Cliff raised his brow. "And why not?" he asked as a sharp whistle came from the direction of the house. At the side of the cabin, Tilly waved an apron as Lavina put her fingers in her mouth and let out another shrill whistle.

Relief filled Milly's face before she ran through the field. "Come Pa, your dinner is ready."

Cliff dropped the hammer into the bucket of staples and hung it on a post. *I guess now is as good a time as any to find out what the girls and Miss Randall have been plotting.*

As Milly ran towards them, Lavina asked, "How did it go?"

Milly shrugged. "He suspects something."

Lavina watched Cliff make his way to the house. "That is fine. I have to ask him anyway. Did you talk me up?"

"Oh yes, I did that good."

Lavina winked at Milly. "That's my girl. You two go on in and pour everyone a glass of milk."

Cliff tipped his hat as he approached.

Speak naturally and for goodness' sake, do not blush. "I improvised a tad, but it looks like a rhubarb and strawberry pie. We will have to see how it tastes."

Cliff stopped at a pipe that ran one hundred feet from a natural thermal and dripped into a bucket. The bucket sat atop a large log with a bar of soap in a dish and a towel on a nail. He scrubbed his hands and said, "I got the impression from Milly you needed to talk to me."

He is not one to dilly-dally. Lavina smoothed her dress. "Why yes. I will make this quick, so your dinner doesn't get cold." She pulled the letter from her pocket and held it out to him. "Ted did not receive my last letter. Apparently, the post office waylaid it."

He dried his hands and peered at the letter. "And what does this have to do with me?"

Lavina cleared her throat and chose her words with caution. "You see, I would hate to leave before Ted's return."

Cliff walked to the door and fanned her through. "What makes you certain he is coming back if he did not receive your letter?" He then pulled her chair out for her.

"The postmaster told me Ted was very disappointed when he didn't receive my letter." She handed him the plate of biscuits.

Tilly pushed a plate with butter on it towards him. "Lavina showed me how to make butter."

That's my girl. Lavina winked at her.

Cliff raised his brow and spread a little butter on his biscuit. He took a bite and mussed Tilly's hair. "Mmm, you did very well."

Tilly blushed, and Milly elbowed her in the ribs. "Lavina is an excellent teacher," she said on cue.

"And Tilly was a tremendous help to me today," Lavina said with a wink.

"You still have not told me why you think Ted will return." Cliff interrupted their act as he continued to eat.

"The postmaster informed me Ted intended to get backers for his mine out east then come back here and try to win my heart." She took a long drink of milk to steady her nerves then said, "So, you see, I cannot leave before we straighten out this little kerfuffle."

"I understand that is what you wish to do." Lavina heard irritation creep into his tone. "What I don't understand is how it concerns me."

Now comes the pitch. Lavina took a deep breath. "There was nothing in town to lease. But I noticed a little outbuilding behind the house." She pointed in its direction and rushed to finish. "I merely need a place to sleep. I will pay for rent and supply my own food."

"There is no chimney coming out of that building and it is so full of junk I couldn't get the door open." His tone was flat.

He ate the last bite of steak, and Lavina was unsure how to proceed. "Yes, I tried as well. But I could clean it out and I saw a cot at the store today amongst the miner's items." She nodded her head at Tilly, who jumped up and retrieved the pie from the windowsill and carried it to her father. "I could cook and clean for y'all and tutor the girls."

Cliff sniffed the pie and winked at Milly. "What a coincidence. Milly was just commenting on her desire for schooling."

Lavina clapped. "Yes, how fortuitous."

Cliff took a bite of pie and nodded his head in approval, but again doused her hopes. "I doubt you could stay warm enough in that building come wintertime."

"Surely Ted will come back before winter." She fidgeted with her fork. "How long could it take to find men willing to invest in a mine that produces both gold and silver?"

"I would not know," Cliff stated as he finished his pie. "That was almost as good as my mother's."

"High praise indeed. Thank you." Lavina could not prevent her nerves from affecting her voice and jumped when Cliff patted her hand.

"Do not fret. I am sure it will not take Ted long to find investors," he said.

Both girls ran and wrapped their arms around Lavina's neck. "Yes, he will come back soon," Tilley said.

Milly placed her hand on her heart. "I swear," she vowed in her thickest southern drawl.

Cliff stood and placed a hand on each girl's shoulder and tugged them from Lavina. "Go catch Maggie girls, she needs to be milked," he said as Lavina started to clear the table.

"I won't kick you out of your bed again tonight." She smiled with discomfort. "I will sleep in the loft with the girls."

"I will stay with my girls." Cliff snapped off each word.

Lavina spun to face him. "No, it's fine. I quite like your young ladies."

He grabbed the milk pail with irritation. "I am not sure how comfortable I am with you getting too close to the girls." He opened the door and in a voice laced with pain, said, "They have had too many women in their lives leave them hurting."

When he walked out the door, he left Lavina in the chill of his anxieties. *He is right. Two months or two years, the pain of being abandoned is very unpleasant indeed.*

The house was back in order when the twins and Cliff carried in the milk. "Get to bed girls, we have a long day tomorrow." He bent and kissed them both.

"Good night, Pa. Good night, Miss Lavina," they said in unison and climbed the ladder.

"Sweet dreams, ladies." Lavina could not prevent melancholy from inserting itself into her statement.

Cliff took out a cheesecloth and held it on a large crock. "Do you mind pouring for me?" he asked.

Lavina lifted the pail and poured the milk over the cloth, then decided to address the issue head-on. "Mister Walters, I would like to ease your mind, if I could."

"On what subject?"

"When my parents died, I inherited a great deal of money. It overjoyed my family to take me in because I came with the money. However, I also came with needs and a slight attitude. They soon found that my attitude was not worth the money and sent me to another greed-filled relative."

Cliff's head came up, and he stared into her eyes. Lavina averted his look of sympathy as she continued her tale. "My assumption that one day they might love me and keep me, caused years of pain. When I accepted the fact, that I would never have these people in my life for more than a year or two, I finally found peace." She set the empty pail on the counter. "I tell you this, to assure you I intend to make it clear to your girls, that my stay here is temporary. I will not fill them with empty promises or dreams of an everlasting relationship." She wiped her hands on her apron and poured a cup of coffee. "Would you care for a cup?"

"Yes. Thank you for that, Miss Lavina." He took the cup she handed him, then continued. "It has been a hard year for us, and I worry for my girls."

They carried their cups to the table and sat. "Tell me about their mother."

Cliff squirmed in his chair. "Not much to tell, really."

Lavina gave him an understanding smile and asked, "Too painful?"

"No, it just seems like a lifetime ago."

"Where did you meet her?

A smile crossed his lips. "We met at a friend's wedding. She was the bridesmaid, and I was the groomsman. We had both traveled a far piece to get there and stayed at the same hotel. I knew the first time I saw her smile she was the one."

Lavina placed her cheek in her hand. “How lovely.”

Cliff stretched out his legs. “I didn’t want to go home without her, so I extended my stay. Before the month was up, I married her.” He straightened back up and drew a hand through his hair. “I thought we would have a long happy life together.”

Lavina could see the pain in his face. “How long were you married?”

“One year, five months, two days, and thirteen hours.” Cliff stood, placed his cup on the counter, and started up the ladder. “I regret nothing, my girls are my world.”

Lavina cleaned their cups, then undressed and crawled under the covers while her thoughts tangled and slithered like worms on a rainy night.

Chapter Five

Cliff woke to the smell of coffee, and two toasty warm girls snuggled against his back. He dressed and carried his boots down the ladder. He placed them on the floor with caution and held his fingers to his lips when Lavina opened her mouth to speak.

"Good morning, Mister Walters," she whispered. Lavina held a spatula in one hand and a pan in the other. She flipped the hot cake in the air and caught it in the skillet as he reached for a coffee cup.

"Before you pour your coffee, do you mind?" She used her elbow to point at the ribbon on the table. "I will eat this pancake. I can see a hair in it."

Cliff picked up the ribbon as she turned toward the stove. *Why would such a beautiful woman marry a man she never met?* With experienced hands, Cliff braided her hair and tied the ribbon at the bottom.

"Thank you. I did not expect you to braid it. But I do appreciate it." She placed the pancake on a plate and pulled out the hair.

Cliff sliced off a pat of butter and smeared it on the cake, then sipped his coffee as he leaned against the counter. "I will hitch up my buckboard for you today and we will go to town for supplies." He pinched off the tip of the leftover pie and tossed it in his mouth.

"That will be nice. Do you want me to heat a piece of pie for you?"

He took the plate with the pancake and sat at the table. "No, there are only two pieces left. Let the girls have them." He then spooned strawberry preserves on the pancake and picked up a fork.

"No." Lavina flipped another cake. "I said I will eat my hair pancake."

Cliff ate it in four bites while Lavina laughed and continued to cook.

Milly covered her sleeping sister's mouth and waited for her eyes to open. She held a finger to her lips and pointed over the loft. When they peeked into the main house, they watched as their father braided Lavina's hair, then scooted to the foot of the bed.

"They look as if they belong together," Milly whispered in her sister's ear. "Tilly, if we work this right, Lavina could be our new Ma."

Tilly shook her head, then sucked on a strand of hair. "I cannot be sneaky."

"You do not need to. You just need not tell on me." Milly put an arm around her sister's shoulder. "You be sweet and helpful to Lavina and I will do the rest. But you cannot give me away." She nodded her head toward the main floor. "Can you do that?"

Tilly pulled her dress over her head with shaky hands and said, "I do not think I can."

She better not ruin this for us. Milly stood and helped Tilly get her arms in the right sleeve. "Listen. Do you like Lavina?"

"Yes," Tilly said as she tugged at her collar.

"You see how much work Pa has to do without grandma. We need to think of him too." *That should convince her.*

Tilly sucked on her hair again. "He does need help."

Milly pulled on her own dress and flipped up her curls. "We need to show Pa, that we need her too. Lavina is good for all of us."

"But Lavina wants to marry Ted," Tilly protested as she buttoned her sister's dress.

"No, she just wants to get married. She's never even met Ted." Milly leaned over and whispered in her sister's ear again, "Now we have little time, so don't mess up things."

"I will try."

Milly hugged her with an evil glint in her eye. "Pa will be so happy with Lavina."

Tilly pulled away and smiled. "I think so too."

Yes, I know you do. Milly followed her sister down the ladder and announced, "Oh, Pa, the house smells so good."

Lavina flipped a pancake. "Thank you, darling. I made a nice, big breakfast. We have much to do today." Lavina put another pancake on Cliff's plate. He had already cleaned up three. She then placed her pan and spatula in the sink and moved the three plates from the counter to the table.

She poured preserves on their pancakes as the girls stared at their father while he ate. Cliff glanced at the twins. "Eat up girls, it's good."

Tilly spoke with confusion. "You did not pray with us, Pa."

Cliff dropped his fork as guilt covered his face.

"I'll pray with you," Lavina said. "I am a Catholic, so we do not hold hands. Y'all can just bow your heads." Lavina made the sign of the cross.

"Bless us O Lord and these thy gifts which we are about to receive through Christ our Lord Amen." She crossed herself again and winked at the girls. "Once y'all finish, I need you to help me wash dishes." Cliff stood to refill his cup and held the pot up as a silent question. "Yes, please," Lavina answered, and he filled her cup as she continued. "Your daddy will hitch the team and take us to town first thing, and I have plenty of cleaning to do before tonight."

"Tonight?" Milly asked and licked her plate.

"Yes, I cannot keep sleeping under the same roof as your daddy. People will talk." She stood and snatched the plate Milly was lapping. "Ladies, do not eat the dishes."

She saw Milly elbow Tilly in the ribs. "What?" Milly frowned at Tilly, then bobbed her head towards their father. "Oh." Tilly lifted her plate and licked it.

Lavina reached over her head and snatched it out of her hand. "You two." She snapped as she poured boiling water over the dishes and handed Tilly a washcloth. "Table." She said then handed Milly the broom. "Floor."

Cliff swallowed the last of his coffee as he stood and walked behind Lavina while she scrubbed dishes. He reached around and dropped the cup in the water and brushed up against her. "Not having to cook this morning was a welcome change, and the meal was excellent. Thank you."

Lavina suppressed a desire to touch the massive peck that rested on her shoulder. "Well you... I mean thank you, no I mean you're welcome." *Oh my goodness, I sound like an idiot.*

Cliff sat in the chair by the ladder and pulled on his boots. "I will be ready in half an hour," he said, then walked out the door. Lavina forgot about the girls and let out a long, loud sigh.

"What is wrong?" Tilly asked.

Lavina jumped and splashed water on the floor. "Nothing, nothing." She stammered, then bent to wipe up the mess. "I was just thinking I should write out a list, so I do not forget anything." She finished the last dish and hurried into Cliff's room, where she threw herself backward on the bed. *Pull it together, Lavina, and move into the shed.* She sat up and pulled out Ted's ad and reread it, then held it to her chest. *Ted. Ted. Ted is why you are here.* She then scribbled out a shopping list, stuffed money in her clutch, and walked back to the primary room. "It shines in here. Come, ladies, let us not keep your daddy waiting."

When Cliff pulled up to the door, Lavina did not climb into the wagon. Instead, she squealed and walked to the front of his horses. "They matched to perfection." She pulled the bridle of the horse closest to her and ran her hand up its nose. "I had a Percheron at my riding club, they are such gentle giants." She winked at the girls. "Kind of reminds me of your daddy."

"They were grandma's horses, she bred them for people to buy," Milly said.

Lavina kissed the horse's muzzle. "Mine was black, I always wanted a dabbled gray. Your grandmother knew her horseflesh, that is certain."

"Pa says he'd have a tough time finding a better pair." Tilly smiled up at her father, who Lavina could see made a heroic effort to appear patient.

She climbed up beside the girls. "Sorry Mister Walker, but my horse was the only thing I regretted leaving behind in Georgia."

When Cliff pulled up in front of the mercantile, Lavina jumped off and helped the girls to the ground. As he set the brake, the proprietor opened the door and greeted her. "Miss Lavina, back so soon?"

Lavina smiled at him and the postmaster as she stepped inside the building. "Yes, I need supplies."

The postmaster slapped his paper in his hand. "So, you have decided to stay?"

"Yes gentlemen, I will stay until Ted returns." She pulled out her list and smiled at the men. "Y'all know my name and now that I will be a fixture in Atlanta, it might be beneficial if I knew yours."

The proprietor waved at the postmaster. "He is Davis Nelson, and I am Carl Burks."

Lavina reached behind her and pulled out the twins. "Let me introduce you to Miss Milly Walters and Miss Tilly Walters." The door closed behind her, and she nodded in Cliff's direction. "And this is their father, Cliff Walters."

The men shook his hand while Lavina continued. "He bought Ted's home. I am renting a hut on the property. So, I will need one of those cots and these supplies." She handed Carl her list. Cliff pulled out a cot while Carl stacked her list of items into crates. "Is there a butcher in town where I can buy fresh meat?"

Davis laughed. "That would be something now, wouldn't it?"

"No ma'am," the proprietor interrupted. "I have canned ham and salt pork."

"Most people hunt their fresh meat," Davis added.

Lavina smiled. "Then I will need a rifle and shells."

Carl glared at him. "Or buy my canned ham and salt pork."

"You can shoot?" The surprised voice came from Milly.

Lavina pulled herself up to her full height and said, "Southern ladies learn to shoot fox while riding sidesaddle at full speed, my dear."

"I have an 1868 Springfield breechloader."

"Perfect. I have shot that rifle plenty. Give me two boxes of 50- 70- 350 cartridges."

"You know your weapons," Carl said as he handed the gun and cartridges to Cliff, who carried them to the wagon.

Lavina leaned a hip against the counter while honey dripped from her lips. "I will also take a couple of your canned hams and two pounds of salt pork. As a child, we ate canned ham every Sunday after mass. It brings back fond memories for me." The proprietor had the look of a hound dog who had found a scent as Cliff reentered and grabbed a crate.

"Can the girls have a peppermint?" Lavina could see their father intended to deny her request and explained, "I want to give it to them as a reward for helping me clean my new home. I won't let them have them until after dinner."

Cliff looked at the girls' excited faces and frowned. "I guess that will be fine."

She took four out of the jar as she directed the girls. "Tilly, you carry out the potatoes while Milly you pack the onions." She winked at them, then asked Carl, "What is the damage?"

"With the rifle, it comes to $93.75." His jaw dropped when Lavina handed him a hundred-dollar bill.

"Another woman of means. Now, why does that not surprise me?" The comment came from the postmaster and irritated Lavina to no end.

Why do people think money is the way to happiness? "I would give up my inheritance to have grown up with parents." She said with more pain than she intended. Silence filled the room and she turned to run headlong into Cliff's broad chest. "Oh goodness. I am sorry."

"No, I am sorry." She heard the sympathy in his voice. *Oh, damn, do not pity me.* He picked up the last crate and followed her out.

As she sat next to the girls on the wagon seat, she could still see pity on Cliff's face and wanted desperately to remove it. She sat up and forced a lilt into her tone. "Ted informed me of a Hot Springs."

"We have been there. We can show you," Milly said.

"Tonight, after we clean, we can go there to bathe."

"Bathe?" the girls moaned in unison.

She gave Cliff her most carefree smile. "Yes, bathe." The girls filled the rest of the uncomfortable trip with complaints and idle chatter.

Chapter Six

At the front door of Cliff's cabin, Lavina jumped down and aided the girls once more. "I will put on a stew for dinner. We can have canned ham, eggs, and biscuits for lunch. You girls can handle that while I find a place for the groceries."

The construction of the counters was rudimentary. Made of raw two-by-four legs, braced bottom and top with four-by-twos and two and two one-by-twelves secured to the top. They ran parallel against two of the kitchen walls, with a wood stove against the other. The kitchen produced no shelves or drawers of any kind for storage.

Lavina set the four crates she had on the counter. *I guess I'll just leave my supplies here.* When she and Tilly snuck a peek into the shed yesterday, they saw pipes and lumber. Plans of how she might make the kitchen more functional ran through her mind. *I cannot wait to get in there and find out what I can use.*

Once Cliff had the horses and wagon put away, he came in for lunch. "I need to finish the fence so I can get the stock out of the corral. The cows fight it every day." He smiled as Lavina placed one piece of pie on his plate and split the other between the girls.

"Of course, which one of you girls will help your daddy, and which one will help me?"

Milly jumped up and stood at her father's elbow. "I will help Pa. We make a good fencing crew."

Cliff mussed her hair and smiled. "You sure made it possible to get the fence good and tight."

Lavina watched the tenderness this giant showed his girls and felt her heart tighten. "And my girl Tilly is quiet and a quick study. So willing to let me jabber on all day."

After Cliff and Milly headed out the door to start their jobs, Lavina sat and frowned at Tilly. "Tilly, you are going to need to learn to be more aggressive like your sister or you'll spend your life doing nothing but housework."

"What is wrong with housework?"

"Bless your heart. The simplicity of your question is precious." Lavina gave her a sympathetic pat on the head as they stood and walked to the shed. "My dear, outside of the kitchen there is a world of possibilities and oodles more excitement."

"But I like housework."

Lavina raised her brows. "I have heard of women like you before." She placed her hip against the shed door and pushed. The sound of metal and wood as it fell caused her to grimace. "Now don't get me wrong, I don't mind housework. But I would rather haul his wood, fix his fence, and hunt his food than wash a man's socks." Lavina pushed the door harder and managed to open it just wide enough for Tilly to slip in.

Tilly handed her the items that had fallen behind the door. "Most of it is pipe, but there is something that looks like twin bathtubs with legs. It fell and I cannot pick it up."

"Keep handing me pipe until I can squeeze in." Once Lavina was inside, they set up the tubs and opened the door wide enough to carry the item out into the sunlight. Lavina clapped. "It is a double sink. It is hideously ugly but infinitely useful."

"Useful?"

"Oh, my little love. For cleaning dishes and washing clothes." Delight filled her voice as she hugged the child's shoulder.

"You're awful excited for someone who hates doing both those things."

Lavina waved her hand in the air. "Well, of course, silly. This will make those jobs easier." She grabbed one side of the sink and motioned to Tilly to do the same. "Which means we can spend less time at the sink and more time doing the things we love."

Tilly picked up the other end and cocked her head. "What kind of things do you love?"

Dreamy memories filled Lavina's head as she answered the innocent question. "Riding horses, hunting, and I love to paint." She pulled Tilly along as she walked backward. "Let's set this in the kitchen by the stove. Then we'll check to see if Ted intended the pipe for drainage and indoor plumbing."

It was a struggle to get the sink into the house. Made with two large, two-foot square blue metal tubs with drain holes and metal legs. Chained to the lip of each tub were metal stoppers.

In the kitchen, Lavina spotted two small boards nailed to the wall by the stove. One was close to the floor, while the other was four feet high. "Oh, see there." She clutched Tilly's hand and hurried outside, where they found two more boards nailed to the outside wall. "Those holes are for the faucet and the drain."

"I can stack the pipe in piles by size and shape." Tilly offered.

"Smart idea. Let's find out what other treasures this shed holds."

When they stepped back in, Lavina realized Ted made the floor out of rock. "That is odd." Wood covered part of the rock and Ted had stacked more against one wall. She assumed the wood on the floor had fallen off the pile. When she picked up the wood and took a step forward, she fell into a hole. "Oh goodness," she yelled as she landed on her bottom.

Tilly ran to help lift the wood off her. "Are you hurt?"

"No," Lavina said then examined the rock-lined hole. "It is a bathhouse."

"A what?"

Lavina stood and dusted off her dress. "A bathhouse." She replaced the board. "Ted had grand plans to use the thermal waters. This incline is a bathtub."

"Oh." Tilly squinched up her little face in her habitual manner.

Lavina smiled and patted her head. "When you get a little older, you will love the luxury of a hot bath." Once they removed the pipe, Lavina informed Tilly the wood needed to stay. "The humidity and weather will warp it. There is plenty of room for my cot and trunk in here. This will suit me fine." The bathhouse was sixteen feet by twelve feet, with no windows and only one door.

"I don't think I could sleep in a place with no windows," Tilly said in her honest way.

Lavina stood back and tapped a finger on her teeth. "You know you are right. I may just have to pull out my art kit and paint windows."

After they set up her cot, they entered the main cabin to unpack her trunk and stir the stew. Lavina pulled out one set of sheets and all her quilts and afghans. "I hope all of them are not necessary to stay warm, but I don't want to regret leaving them in here while I freeze out there."

She handed Tilly her pillow and sheets and gathered her blankets. Once they made her bed, they gathered the items she left in Cliff's bedroom. She placed them on the stack of wood and dusted off her hands. "Well Tilly Shy, until your daddy can move my trunk, we are finished in here."

They exited the shed, gathered up the pipe they decided belonged with the sink, and carried it inside while Cliff and Milly meandered their way home through the field. Lavina placed her armload of pipe in the sink and opened her trunk. She pulled out four of her China soup bowls. "I am not in the mood to chase soup around a tin plate."

Tilly laughed, then eyed the bowls with admiration. "Those are beautiful."

"Thank you, they were my mother's."

"Our Mama died when we were born."

Lavina stroked the child's head. "My momma and daddy died when I was three years old. I have no actual memories of them. But I always feel them with me." She stirred the stew, then changed the subject. "Will you put the bread and butter on the table?"

Lavina scraped the cream off the morning milk into a jar and added salt, then handed it to Tilly to shake. She then poured four glasses of milk and huffed. "What a waste."

"What is the problem?" Cliff's voice made her jump.

"You need a cat, or a dog, or pigs. Far too much milk is being thrown out," she said without thinking.

Milly squealed, "Can we get a dog?" while Tilly pleaded, "No Pa, a cat." Cliff glared at Lavina.

Really Lavina, when are you going to learn to keep your mouth shut? "I am sorry." She ignored the girls' hound dog faces. "Of course, cats and dogs are out of the question. Between the bears and coyotes, you couldn't keep one alive long enough to be of much use. A pig would be more sensible. You can have ham and bacon and pork chops." She picked up the ladle with a shaky hand and continued with her ramblings. "Pickled pig feet are delicious," she said as she ladled soup in the four bowls. "I have a cousin who raised pigs. He says you can eat everything except the squeal."

Lavina sat beside Cliff, reached across the table to hold Milly's hand as he held hers, and prayed in his deep timbre. She shook a lustful thought to the back of her mind as the heat of his skin transferred to hers. *Goodness Lavina, he is praying, what will your sainted grandmother think?*

Cliff raised his head and pointed to the sink. "Was that in the shed?"

Lavina stood. "Oh. Oh, yes." She pulled out the faucet. "And the fittings for plumbing." She sat back down and clapped. "Also, the shed is a bathhouse, it has no plumbing either, but a rock-lined tub and the fixtures." She took a bite of soup. "You girls do not realize what a luxury it will be."

Excitement crossed Cliff's face for the first time tonight. "How big is the tub?"

"Big enough for a giant." The girls giggled at her statement.

"That will be a luxury indeed," Cliff said with a deep, dimpled smile.

Heat rose in Lavina's cheeks as she drove out another disturbing thought that added a fearful stammer to her words. "I was wondering about using it to heat the shed at night. A constant flow of scalding water should make a nice furnace. What do you think?"

Cliff nodded his head. "It might work, but I am not sure how strong the sulfur smell can get in a shed that small."

"Hum. No, I hadn't thought of that. You are probably right. I best not attempt it."

The girls ate in silence, and Lavina could not pinpoint the reason for their scrutiny of Cliff and herself. "Mister Walters, if you have clothes you need to be washed the girls and I will take them with us when we go to bathe." Lavina then witnessed a hopeful look pass between the girls.

"I will wash my own," Cliff said in a monotone that made the girls' faces change back into a pout. "Looks as if you ruined that dress today," he added.

"Yes, all of my clothes are inappropriate for what it takes to live in the Rocky Mountains." She winked at the girls. She hoped her tease might bring them out of their moping. "I was thinking I should go to town and buy a couple of bolts of material and make clothes that I can do *stuff* in. Maybe the girls can come pick out a bolt they like, and I will sew them new dresses as well." The girls' expressions changed to fear, and Lavina turned to face Cliff.

He cut his eyes at her with ominous slits. "Until we get the fence built and I pick up work, frills are not in the budget."

Oh, goodness. I've done it again. When will I learn to think before I speak? Lavina ignored the girls as they hung their heads and moaned. "Will you be working for one of the larger mines?"

Cliff stood and refilled his bowl before he replied. "At times, for cash money, but mostly I will trade for work."

"Trade? Trade work for what?"

"For silver."

"And what will you do with the silver?"

Both girls pulled back their sleeves to reveal matching silver bracelets. Lavina leaned in closer. The items gave the appearance of lace dipped in silver. "Lovely," she breathed.

"When I get my forge set up, I can start doing what I love again."

Lavina stared at him in awe. "You are an artist. These are absolutely beautiful."

"Thank you."

Lavina examined the details of the bracelets again. "Do you have any other samples? I would love to send a sample to a jeweler friend I have in Atlanta. He has nothing as lovely as these."

"I have a couple of pieces."

"I will search my trunk for a box to mail them, along with a letter. He is an honest man. I trust him with my life. He is my godfather."

Cliff reached out and cupped her hand. "I will be grateful for that."

From the corner of her eye, Lavina watched as the girl's smiles returned.

After they cleaned up dinner and the girls gathered their dirty clothes, Lavina asked Cliff for a lantern. "To find our way home if it gets too dark."

Cliff handed her a lantern and a box of wooden matches, then walked into his room and came out with two towels.

"I almost forgot." Lavina opened her trunk and took out a bar of soap, a towel, cream dentifrice, and a toothbrush. "Will you help me move my trunk when I get back?"

Cliff locked the lid, grabbed the handle, and swung the heavy trunk to his shoulder while Lavina ran ahead to open the doors. As he placed it by the foot of her bed, he knelt and lifted a board covering the hole in the floor. "Pretty good masonry."

"Yes, I have not met Ted yet and become more impressed with him every day." Cliff cocked his head, and Lavina got the impression his black eyes searched her mind for signs of instability. "Humph." She removed her clothes from the pile of wood and backed out the door. "Are you ready, girls?"

Milly and Tilly ran out to meet her, and the three of them started their stroll across the field. Five yards from the cabin, Tilly stepped in excrement. "Yuck! What is it?" she squealed as she lifted her foot.

Lavina bent and examined it closer. "It is bear scat."

Tilly's entire body shook as she screamed, "It's still warm."

Lavina stood and glanced around but did not see any sign of a bear. She peered at the scat again. "Looks as if he has been eating wild onions. Tomorrow we will have to track him and find his cash." She kissed Tilly's frightened cheek. "But tonight, we are going back to get your daddy and a gun."

Chapter Seven

As Cliff loaded Lavina's new rifle, a tightening in his chest increased. Lavina asked him to guard them while they bathed. He was incapable of stopping the growing attraction to this woman, and this job was in no way a deterrent.

He also sensed his girls were becoming attached to Lavina much faster than he thought possible. *I don't need this in my life.* As he observed the girls talking to Lavina at the kitchen table, he grew irritated. "Ready when you are." He slung the gun over one shoulder while Tilly grabbed his free hand.

"I missed you today, Pa." He bent and picked her up as they headed to the thermals.

"I missed you too, my sweet Tilly girl." Cliff had worked, cleaned, cooked, and rested with both his girls in tow their entire lives and missed them when they were not with him.

A couple of hundred yards from the house, Lavina stopped in her tracks and stared. From a thirty-foot cliff flowed a waterfall that thermal springs fed from higher ground. Early settlers had stacked rocks into a circle at the base to make what the locals called Chattanooga Hot Springs.

Cliff placed Tilly on her feet beside Lavina. "Impressive, isn't it?"

"Oh, goodness yes." She winked at the twins. "Now I know you're tempted to run and jump in to get yourselves clean and scrubbed." Cliff smiled at the looks on the girls' faces as Lavina teased them. "But first we will wash our clothes."

Milly handed Cliff and Tilly their clothes. They removed their shoes and socks, and Cliff put cuffs on his pants. He pulled off his shirt to wash it, along with one other and a pair of pants. The girls only brought the dresses they wore, underclothes, and two pairs of wool stockings. Lavina washed three each of dresses, pantaloons, camisoles, stockings, and a corset.

When Cliff finished his washing, he picked up his bar of soap and walked to the falls. He detected Lavina's eyes on him as he scrubbed his head with the soap, then lathered his neck, arms, and chest.

He kept an eye on the girls as they strolled up to Lavina while she ogled him open-mouthed. Her head snapped in the girl's direction. "Come now ladies, it's rude to stare."

He sauntered their way as Milly said, "You were staring at Pa."

Lavina blushed and started scrubbing her last item. "Pish, I was not."

Cliff stepped onto the bank as Tilly gave her an indignant look. "You were too. We both saw you."

When Lavina looked up, Cliff stood a few feet in front of her as a smile spread across his lips. She waved her hand in the air. "Nonsense. I was admiring his belt buckle. Did you make it?"

"Yes, he did. See how pretty." The girls each clutched an arm and pulled him to within inches of Lavina as she sat. This left her eye to buckle with Cliff. She slid backward off her rock and scrambled to her feet. "Yes, yes, very, the silverwork is lovely." She rushed behind a bush. "It is late, girls. Let us bathe."

Cliff mussed the girl's hair. "You heard her," he said, then walked fifteen feet away and sat on a rock with his back to them, rifle in hand.

Lavina threw her dress over the bush and walked out in her pantaloons and camisole. Milly and Tilly were naked and sat on the rocks, washing the underclothes they had removed. "Aren't you going to wash your dress?" Milly asked.

"I won't have anything dry to wear home."

"We just walk home in our towels." The girls laid their clothes on rocks and waded into the pool.

Lavina stepped in and waded knee-deep to the falls. Milly asked, "Why don't you take off your underclothes?"

The heat rose in Lavina's cheeks. "Well, not that your daddy would look intentionally, but if he were obliged to glance our way, I am more comfortable in my underclothes."

"How will you wash your skin?" Tilly asked.

Lavina rolled her eyes and stepped into the falls. "I will manage, just you never mind." As the water ran over her undergarments, they became a second skin and hid nothing from Cliff's view if, as she said, he happened to look. She stepped out and applied soap to her hair. When she leaned back to rinse it out, the girls let out a blood-curdling scream. Lavina looked to where they had been playing and saw a big brown bear on its hind legs five yards in front of them.

She ran between the girls and screamed, "RUN!" As the girls ran out of the water, Lavina squared off with the bear. He swiped at the air, shook his head, and let out a roar. Lavina stood her ground. The adrenaline pumping in her ears drowned out the world around her until a shot rang out. Lavina jumped, and the bear dropped to all fours, spun, and ran into the trees.

Her legs could no longer support her weight, and she crumpled into the pool. Cliff put an arm behind her back and slammed her tight against his chest. "Thank you, thank you!" he repeated as he held her captive.

Milly and Tilly rushed behind her and hugged her back. They too thanked her as tears streaked their faces. Lavina stuck her chin in Cliff's chest and pushed her nose high. "I can't breathe," she gasped.

Cliff loosened his hold. "That was brave or stupid. Either way, I can't thank you enough."

"Pish. I was just hoping he might show us to the onion patch, then you had to go and scare him away."

He pulled her to his chest again. "Don't do that."

"Do what?" Innocence was not one of Lavina's strong points.

Cliff pulled her tighter. "Don't act as if it was nothing." His voice cracked as he released his grip and gazed into her eyes. "I cannot take another loss in my life." Lavina heard the pain behind his words and softened her look. "They are my world, and you will let me thank you for saving their lives."

"Oh, uh." Lavina's chin quivered. "You're welcome, Mister Walters."

"Daddy, I want to go home," Tilly said.

"Please Daddy, let's get out of here," Milly pleaded along with her sister.

The girls wrapped their towels around themselves while Cliff stood and pulled Lavina to her feet then told her, "Wrap in a towel. I will gather our clothes."

Lavina led the way home as she tried to cover her fear of meeting with another bear. "This will haunt our dreams tonight," she said and held the lantern high while Milly and Tilly walked behind her and Cliff brought up the rear.

"What's with calling me, daddy?" Cliff teased the girls.

Milly shrugged. "Lavina does."

"She calls me Daddy?" Lavina could detect the cringe in his voice.

Milly mimicked Lavina's drawl. "Your daddy needs help. Your daddy said no. Your daddy has a nice belt buckle."

Lavina slapped her forehead as the girls giggled. *Oh goodness, I need to go to bed and start this day over.*

When they reached the house, Lavina held the door open while Cliff walked in and lit another lantern. She bent and whispered to the girls. "You best watch your tongue Milly Sly, or I'll feed you to that bear myself." She hugged them to her and teased, "Sweet dreams, darlings. I'm glad you're not bear poop."

Milly hugged her neck tight. "I love you, Miss Lavina."

Lavina swallowed her tears and stared into Cliff's face while Tilly kissed her cheek. "I love you too, Miss Lavina."

"I love you too, girls." She swallowed her tears, then stood and walked to her shed.

Once he got the girls calmed and they fell asleep, Cliff climbed down the ladder and snuffed out the lantern. Light from outside caught his attention. When he looked out the window, he saw Lavina squatting in front of the hot water pipe, struggling to rinse the soap out of her hair.

He grabbed a kitchen chair and a bucket and walked to her. "Sit here and let me help." He placed the bucket under the drip of warm water.

Lavina was still in her wet underclothes. She sat in the chair and pulled her towel over her breast. "Thank you. I didn't get the soap out in the terror of the moment."

Cliff squatted and touched the water with his fingers. "Understandable. A bucket should make this easier," he said as he picked up the full bucket of water. "Ready?"

Lavina flipped her hair over the back of the chair. "Yes."

With care, Cliff poured the water with one hand and ran his fingers through her hair with the other. "It will take at least one more bucket. I have never seen so much hair."

"Thank you."

"It wasn't a compliment, just an observation."

Lavina snickered. "Well then, you are very observant Mister Walters."

That was a stupid thing to say. You sounded like an ass!

He searched for something to say when Lavina cleared her throat. "I understand you will be busy tomorrow, but do you mind if I try to plumb the bathhouse? I am sure the girls will appreciate it after tonight's scare."

"You're not worried about the aroma?" He poured the second bucket as he worked the soap out of her hair.

"There are taps and drains. I don't need to use it for heat. We can drain it after each use."

Cliff no longer felt soap in her hair, but sat the bucket on the ground to fill again. "Speaking of heat, I started a fire for the girls." His voice sounded awkward, even to himself. "They were chilled walking home. You can come sit by it to dry your hair and clothes."

"Thank you." She ran her fingers through her hair. "I think you got all the soap."

Yes, I know. I was hoping to think of a compliment that didn't sound forced. He nodded. "I'll take in the chair if you'll grab the lantern."

"You never answered my question."

Cliff searched his mind for the question she asked as he had been distracted by his foolish remark. "Oh, yes. It shouldn't take long tomorrow to finish the fence. If you gather everything you think we need, I can dig trenches and connect the pipe." He placed the chair close to the fireplace, then moved the cold coffee to the heat. Cliff smelled the bucket of milk on the counter and grimaced, then threw it out the door while Lavina tried to dry her hair. She was having trouble keeping her breasts covered enough for modesty and getting the job done. Cliff picked up one of the girl's towels, which he had hung over the back of the kitchen chairs.

"Thank you." There was a trimmer in her voice as he began to dry her hair. "We need to find a way to use more milk."

"What do you suggest?" He smiled at her effort to cover her obvious nervousness at his proximity.

"Well, other than butter, I have no recipes that call for copious amounts of milk. I suppose I can make more cream-based soups."

"I will appreciate that." He ran his fingers through her hair. It was dry. He poured two cups of coffee and scooped a spoonful of cream in each one, then handed it to Lavina.

She took a sip. "Mmm, I could get used to that."

Cliff could hear the girls as they whispered to each other. "What's wrong now?" he yelled in the direction of the loft.

Milly poked her head over the rail. "Tilly had a bad dream. She is crying."

His tone softened, "Tilly, do you want to sleep in my bed?"

"Yes, Pa." She jumped out of bed and started down the ladder.

"Can I too Pa, please?" Milly asked.

"Yes, come down and snuggle in."

Tilly hit the floor and turned to Lavina. "Did you have a bad dream too?"

Milly ran to Lavina and pulled on her arm. "Come on. Pa has a gigantic bed. You can snuggle in with us."

"Can she, Pa?" Tilly hugged his arm.

Cliff and Lavina spoke together. "I am fine." "She would not want that."

He stood and gathered their cups as Lavina sorted through the clothes on the table. "You girls go to bed now," he said to fill the discomfort of the girls' invitation.

Lavina placed her clothes over her arm, then stepped out the door. "Goodnight, my loves."

Cliff placed a hand on the wood of the door and sighed then followed the girls to his bed and pulled off his boots.

"Was she talking to you too, Pa? Are you her love?"

It had been years since he had thought of love. The girl's mother was young and pretty, but frail and scared. Lavina was a mature, strong, brave woman with jaw-dropping beauty. "She was talking to you. Lavina has promised herself to another man, she doesn't need me."

The girls moved to either side of the bed to force Cliff to sleep between them. Tilly snuggled into his chest and said in her honest way, "He might not come back."

Milly popped up her head. "Yeah, Pa, what if he doesn't come back? Can you be her love then?"

Cliff chuckled. "Ted not coming back does not make her mine nor will it make her love me."

"Well, can't you make her love you?" Milly pleaded.

"You can't make someone love you. Now lay down and go to sleep."

Tilly sat up once more. "She told me Ted's letters made her come here to marry him."

"What does that have to do with me?" Annoyance now filled his voice.

"Maybe you should write her love letters."

"She lives in the shed outback. I don't need to write to her. I can walk out the door and talk to her any time I need to."

Milly sat up once more. "But Pa, you don't talk, you grunt."

"Enough girls." He pulled both girls onto their backs. "Go to sleep, now!"

Milly moaned. "See Pa, that is not talking."

"Shush up."

When he closed his eyes, a vision of Lavina in her clinging, wet underclothes filled his thoughts. He remembered her breast against his chest and his arm in the crook of her back. *It felt so right... And she has promised herself to another, you fool!* Cliff shook his head, rolled over, and willed himself to sleep.

Chapter Eight

It was an instinct to put herself between the girls and the bear. *But goodness, how could I not fall in love with two such little darlings?*

The heat from Cliff's touch as he helped wash her hair spread as if wildfire ran through her veins. In her shed, Lavina doused it with cold water when she pulled out Ted's letters.

She closed her eyes and again a preview of Cliff's brawny chest as he lathered it in the falls lept to the front of her mind. The show his rippling abs put on caused her breath to cease.

She shook her head. "I am here for Ted." She cupped her face. "I am here for Ted." She threw herself back on her pillow. "Oh, pish! I am here for Ted."

Lavina tossed and turned, prayed and worried. When these failed, she got up from her bed and dug out her painting supplies. As she looked at the walls, windows did not scream out at her. The vision that came to her mind was a naked Grecian-style woman with a vase on her shoulder pouring water into the tub.

She took out a black pastel and drew a life-sized outline of what she would later fill in with paint. From the corner of her eye on the wall above her bed, her artistic mind made out of a rock in the wood. She outlined the rock and sketched three more naked women, one sitting on the rock with her back to the room. Another she had stretched out on the ground with her arms folded on the rock as she laid her cheek on them. The last woman stood in all her glory, unbinding her floor-length hair.

Her lack of a window gave no indication of time, and Lavina was now on a mission. The wood stacked against the opposite wall prevented her from drawing women in standing positions, so Lavina changed tactics. *Once I remove the wood, I can draw a chaise lounge.* For now, she drew a naked woman who appeared to have fainted while two servants stood over her with ostrich feather fans.

Lavina knelt on the woodpile, putting the last touches on one servant boy's collar when a knock came on her door. "Come in."

Cliff entered with a cup of coffee in his hand. "You didn't come to breakfast. I was beginning to worry."

Lavina dusted off her hands and climbed down from the pile of wood. "Is it morning?"

Cliff scanned the room. "I'm guessing you didn't sleep last night."

The color burned into Lavina's cheeks as she took the cup of coffee out of his hand. "No, I was... Well, you see, I started out... I started with the idea to paint windows, to make it cheerier in here. But then I saw a vision. And that vision morphed into what you see now." Lavina took a swallow of her coffee as Cliff open-mouth-gazed around the room.

Oh, dear, he hates it. I should have asked him first. "It's just chalk. It's not paint. I can wash it right off. I'm sorry I should have spoken with you first." *Why doesn't he say something?* Lavina picked up a towel and started wiping off her first drawing.

Cliff grabbed her hand. "No! I didn't say I didn't like it. It's fine." A smile crossed his lips as his cheeks dished into enormous dimples. "Miss Randall, I apologize for how selfish I've been. I should have given my room to you and taken the shed myself. But we can rectify that now."

Lavina laughed and slapped his chest. "Oh yes, terribly selfish of you. I see I am going to need to paint clothes on my ladies."

Cliff threw back his head and laughed. "No need to do anything so drastic."

"Fine, clothes it is." She looked around the room. "Sorry, my lovelies, but your days of frolicking nude are short-lived." She turned and headed to the house. "Come, Mister Walker, it's time to say goodbye to the dream that was."

Cliff followed her out and suggested, "You could paint them in sheer nightgowns."

It was Lavina's turn to laugh out loud. "Or I can paint them wearing gunny sacks."

This morning Tilly volunteered to work with her father while Milly and Lavina laid out pipe and fittings for the bathhouse. Milly's frown, which she wore most of the day, told Lavina how she felt about the drawings.

When they removed the wood from her shed, Lavina found a stack of clippings like the one she possessed. They had the dates of six consecutive years and different ad numbers, with similar poetry.

These are creepy, and mine is not here. She peered closer at the first ad, then dropped them. She pulled hers out of her purse and picked the others off the floor. As she knelt beside her cot, she laid them on the bed while a shiver ran the full length of her spine. They bore a similar hand-drawn heart.

Oh my goodness, how many women came to this remote location to marry Ted? And how many made it out alive? "What a fool I am."

Milly peered over her shoulder. "What is wrong, Miss Lavina?"

Lavina stood and stuffed the advertisements in her purse. "Nothing sugar, we need to start lunch. Your daddy will be hungry soon."

Lunch was a delicious creamy potato soup with bread and thick butter. She served a custard of sorts for dessert. "I never made custard before, so you must make suggestions what y'all think might improve it." Lavina's consisted of milk, eggs, vanilla, brown sugar, and cornstarch.

"You should have put fruit in it," Tilly said.

"No," Milly contradicted. "She should have made them with pastries like grandma and..."

Cliff ate his in three bites. "Delicious. I could eat it at every meal. Thank you, Miss Randall."

Lavina straightened in her seat and smiled. "You're welcome, Mister Walker.

Tilly rolled her eyes. "Pa, she saved our lives. Call her Lavina."

Cliff put his plate in the sink while he explained to the girls, "That is not the way it works. Neither she nor her family has given me that liberty."

Lavina stood and made a small curtsy. "Call me, Lavina."

Cliff chuckled and bowed over her hand. "Call me, Cliff."

"Hot water please, Cliff," Lavina said as she handed him the pail, then moved the washbasin from the counter to the table. "Can you girls clean up our lunch, while your daddy and I work on the plumbing? If we work hard, we might have a new kitchen sink tonight."

Cliff poured the water over the dishes and followed Lavina outside. When they entered the bathhouse, she opened her purse and removed the ads. "What do you make of these?"

He read the clippings and handed them back. "He sure has been persistent in his pursuit of a wife."

Lavina fanned them out and pointed out the heart on each one. "You don't think that is disturbing."

Cliff shrugged. "I am sure he assumed each one might bring love."

"No, no. This one was not with the others. It is mine, and I drew the heart. I am certain the women drew all the hearts."

Cliff took them from her again. "Hum, what's going through your mind?"

Lavina rubbed between her eyes and howled, "That I should look around for shallow unmarked graves."

"Ha, you don't really think that."

"No, not really. But there has got to be something wrong with Ted. Six women came out here looking for the man of their dreams and left disappointed."

"What of the lifestyle? This is a harsh, lonely country. I am surprised you've stayed this long. I have asked myself a hundred times why a beautiful, wealthy woman from high society might come here to live a life of demanding work and hardship."

"I suppose I am experiencing the same euphoria the first fur trapper felt when he saw the Rockies and never moved back to civilization. A sense of belonging, a sense that I am home."

"You didn't have to be a mail-order bride, to find that."

"I wanted something different, something exciting. Ted's letters made it sound so perfect. Now I wonder if he gets a perverse pleasure in having women fall for him only to run away from them."

"Why might he do that?"

Lavina covered her eyes. "I don't know. Maybe I am imagining things, but I pride myself on being different and now look." She tapped the clippings with her finger. "I am as big a fool as all of them. And here I sit, in a shed, waiting for someone who... who... What? I don't know what! Why would he do this?"

"We are finished. How can we help?" Milly's voice made Lavina jump.

"I will start digging the drain line," Lavina said as she hurried past them. "You girls stay and help your daddy."

Cliff raised his brows at Milly and Tilly, then stuffed the ads in his shirt pocket. "I will stay inside and attach the tap while you push the pipe through on the outside. You need to hold it tight and don't let it move."

Cliff worried over Lavina most of the day. *I hope she waits to hear from Ted before making another rash decision.*

When Lavina walked in to cook dinner, she had a bathhouse, and they were putting the finishing touches on the kitchen sink. She tried her hand at custard-filled eclairs that received glowing reviews.

"After two days of sweat and dirt, I will just burn this dress," she commented as she pulled off her apron.

"No," Milly yelled. "It's so pretty."

"Pretty isn't practical. But I guess I will try to clean it since staying here is not practical either."

Both Milly and Tilly screamed, "No, you can't leave us. You promised to teach us things."

Cliff watched as his girls encircled Lavina and repeated her promises back to her.

Lavina pounded the table. "Stop! You don't understand. You could never understand." The girls pulled back in shock as she stomped out the door.

Cliff called them to him. "She has had a long day. Now let's clean up and go to bed."

"Is she going to leave, Pa?" Milly asked.

"I don't know."

Tilly put their plates in the sink and turned on the tap. "Maybe she just needs a good cry."

"Perhaps, baby girl."

"Or she might be crazy," Milly said.

"What makes you say that."

"Why else did she draw naked ladies all over her house?"

Cliff laughed. "Oh, that. Well, in big cities they have communal bathhouses. Lots of people go there and bathe together."

"Yuck." Tilly grimaced.

Milly furrowed her brow. "That doesn't explain why Miss Lavina drew naked ladies everywhere."

"On the walls of the bathhouses are murals similar to those Lavina drew," Cliff explained.

"Have you ever been to one, Pa?" Tilly asked.

"No. But I have heard stories." Cliff mussed Tilly's hair. "Go on now. No more questions. You girls need to get to bed."

"I still think she is crazy." Milly rolled her eyes. "She mumbled under her breath all day about where she might bury a body. I like her and all, but I don't want to wake up dead."

Cliff hugged the girls to him. "She was not talking about burying us. She just has a silly idea concerning Ted."

"Ted? Did she kill him?" Milly's voice was high-pitched. "Is that why he doesn't come back?"

"Good grief, how did we get here? Your imaginations are as bad as Lavina's. No one killed anyone and buried them in the yard." Cliff popped the girls on their bottoms. "I swear women, no matter what their age, have crazy notions. Now get up to bed."

Once the girls were in bed, Cliff blew out the lantern and peered out the window. *Now that the fence and house are in order, I need to find work.*

The next morning, Cliff woke up early and made coffee. He ate a leftover éclair and wrote a note.

Miss Lavina,

I have gone to town to look for work.
Girls,
Be good and do not get underfoot.

Chapter Nine

Cliff met with disappointment at the mines. Three of the large mines had ground to a halt two years earlier to await a solution for the recovery problems. Silver ore was refractory and recovering the gold from the ore was not economical. The Monarch Mill used the natural Hot Springs to run their turbines during the long, harsh winters and turned out high-grade rock in limited amounts for their Indiana owners.

Cliff headed out to look for work at one of the small privately owned mines. A large man pushed a wheelbarrow out of a dark mine entrance as Cliff approached. "Hello, I am looking for honest work," Cliff said as he removed his hat.

The wiry redhead's green eyes scrutinized him. "Damn man, you are a giant." He shook Cliff's hand. "You've come none too soon. I'm Randy Glascock. My brother and I own this mine. He is home with our mother. She broke her ankle, and we take turns staying home with her. I hoped to hire a man, but in you, I'd have a crew. Can you swing a pick?"

"Yes, sir. I've done my share of mining in Montana."

"I didn't think I recognized you from around here." Randy gave him a dubious squint. "What do you want for wages?"

"I had hoped to trade for silver, but I understand that is out of the question."

"No chance there, and we can't afford much more than jawbone wages. However, that is all you're going to get anywhere else in these parts. We usually do the work ourselves, and with our mother hurt this time of year, we might not be able to pay you that much."

"I take it you're not running a year-round operation?"

"Ground frost limits our mining abilities. It freezes hard here, and if we don't get enough ore out in time, it will be a long hungry winter."

"My twin girls could help take care of your mother. That will allow the three of us to pull out enough ore to fill our bellies this year."

Randy wiped a blackened hand across his sweaty forehead and grimaced. "We couldn't afford to pay the girls."

Cliff concentrated for a moment, then grabbed a shovel and pick. "What do you say to this? The three of us work the mine for the season and you give me a quarter of the profits. That way each of you gets a quarter, and a quarter goes back into your operation." Randy scratched his head and appeared to be warming to the idea. "That means no out-of-pocket wages for the season," Cliff said to add extra enticement to the deal.

The man rubbed his chin and squinted. "You have a deal, giant." He thrust out a calloused hand. "Grab a wheelbarrow and let's make some money."

"You can call me Cliff, Cliff Walters."

Randy threw back his head. "Ha. Your mama had a premonition when she gave you that name."

Lavina pocketed Cliff's note and started breakfast for the girls. As she ladled cream into her coffee, an idea occurred to her. "Who's going to milk the cow?"

"Pa does, every morning and night." Milly's answer startled Lavina.

"Oh girls, you are awake." She opened the oven and took out her soufflé. "Your father left a note saying he went to search for work. Do either of you know how to milk a cow?"

"Yes," Tilly huffed. "But we take forever."

Lavina sat with her coffee and ate. "I can help if you teach me."

"We can do it by ourselves."

Lavina was unsure why Milly seemed to be acting extra cold to her this morning. "I should learn in case your father finds a job."

Milly shrugged. "Do as you like."

I wonder what I've done now to upset her.

Lavina's help did not decrease the time it took to milk and furthermore irritated the cow. Her tugging the tits instead of squeezing caused the cow to kick at the bucket. "Well, this is a fine how-do-you-do," Lavina screamed as milk covered them. "I guess this gives us a good excuse to use our new bathhouse."

Milly cut her eyes at Lavina and told Tilly, "I bet she did it on purpose just to make us bathe."

Lavina's head snapped in the child's direction. "Milly sly, you possess as much sass as that cow."

Drenched in milk, the three released the cow and sloshed into Lavina's shed to draw a bath.

"You two bathe first," Lavina said as she filled the tub with water. "Then I will bathe, and afterward we can wash our clothes." Lavina turned her back on the girls, stripped out of her milk-soaked dress, and pulled on her dressing gown.

"You're right," Tilly said as she crawled into the warm water. "This is nicer than walking to the falls every time we need a bath."

Lavina smiled and handed the girls her soap. "And no bears in here."

"Nope," Milly said. "Just strange naked women staring at us while we are naked."

What has gotten into her today? "Well, Miss Milly, I have an idea to fix that." Lavina sat and brushed the tangles from the girls' hair. "I have sheer material. After I paint them, I can drape the material over them to give my painting a two-dimensional look."

"That sounds crazy to me." Milly snapped.

Lavina furrowed her brow, then pulled out a length of sheer cloth and held it over her drawing. "I will make it look as if they are wearing clothes."

"That will be pretty." Tilly clapped. "Can we help?"

"I would appreciate that." Lavina watched as Milly's smile returned. "I guess I'm not so crazy anymore?" Lavina said as she kissed the child's head.

"Depends." Milly's tone was thick with snark as she pulled away. "Are you still looking for a place to bury a body?"

"What?" Lavina asked in shock, then recalled Milly staring at her with fear yesterday. "Oh, darling." She giggled and knelt to meet Milly's eye. "Don't listen to my ramblings. I got a silly idea that Ted may have killed and buried one of his other mail-order brides."

Milly flinched away from her hand. "So, you are both crazy!"

"No, no. I didn't say he did, I said I thought he did."

"If you think that, why are you waiting for him to come back?" Milly asked with a voice full of disgust as the color drained from Tilly's face.

"Yeah, what if he does that to you?"

"He is not going to." Lavina laughed. "I told you I was just rambling. Besides, your daddy's here, I need not fear anyone."

The girls were silent as they wrapped in towels and headed out the door. Lavina stepped into the tub when Milly stuck her head back in the bathhouse. "You might want to think good and hard about what you just said concerning our Pa before you go marrying a man you don't know."

The depths of the child's word burned into Lavina's brain with its precision.

After lunch, Lavina and the girl sat at the table and made lesson plans for their education. The girls wore only their underclothes while their dresses dried by the fire.

With her head laid on the table, Tilly watched Lavina with a slight smile that was unnerving. "What is on your mind, Tilly Shy?"

Tilly reached out and fingered the lesson plan. "Does this mean you'll stay?"

Lavina took a deep breath and let it out in one long sigh. "Regardless of whether I stay, you need an education. This plan will help your father as well."

Milly's voice filled with anger. "So, you are going to leave?"

A sudden wave of exhaustion swept over Lavina. "Listen, ladies. It's best if you settle it in your minds that I am merely here on loan. That I am leaving, but that we can still be friends."

"How can we be friends if you leave?" Milly's voice raised to reveal her irritation.

Tilly whispered her reply with no effort to hide her pain. "You'll never come back."

Lavina stood to shake off her uneasiness at their conversation and gathered her notebook. "You will learn to read and write, and we will send letters to one another." She laid the items on the desk. "Now let's make a nice big dinner for your poor working daddy."

"Why don't you marry Pa?" Milly shouted in frustration.

A sharp knife cuts the quickest. Lavina faced the girls and told them the hard truth. "Because I made a promise to Ted that I will wait for him. Plus, your daddy is not looking for a wife. I am sure he is eager for me to leave so y'all can get your lives back." Lavina pulled Tilly off her chair where she slouched. "You can peel potatoes while your sister cuts up carrots. We will make a hearty stew and bread."

The girls moped the entire time as they helped prepare dinner and grumbled nonstop during the second milking of the cow. It was well after dark when Lavina heard Cliff's footsteps on the porch.

"Smells delicious," he said as he opened the door. Lavina watched with admiration as he picked up the girls and kissed them each in turn. "Ah, my reasons for living. How was your day?"

"Lavina helped us milk the cow," Milly said.

"Then she made us take a bath," Tilly added.

Milly glared at her and continued, "Lavina let us peel potatoes and carrots."

"She also made us wash clothes and do the dishes."

Lavina laughed aloud, noting how every time Milly said she helped them, Tilly pointed out how she made them do something unpleasant. *I have my suspicions about what they are up to, but they are working against themselves.*

Cliff carried them to their chairs and kissed their heads. "Yes, yes. Let me wash up and you can tell me of your day during dinner." He stepped back onto the porch, pulled his shirt over his head, and slapped it against his pant legs.

Lavina stared at his rippling muscles while dirt flew up around him. He hung the filthy shirt on a nail and stomped his boots. "I don't want to mess up the clean floor Lavina made you mop." He mussed Tilly's hair with one large hand.

At the sink, Cliff lathered his arms, chest, and face with soap, then leaned over it to rinse. The whole while Lavina stared with her lips parted. When he turned and sat on the edge of the sink to dry himself with a hand towel, he asked, "What smells so good?"

No sound permeated Lavina's hearing until the girls giggled. She jumped, grabbed a bowl, and ladled up their dinner. "Stew, sorry, we made stew and bread."

The smile on Cliff's lips as he stood and folded the towel made his dimples appear and caused Lavina's knees to buckle. "Nothing as satisfying as a good meal after a long day." He laid the towel on the counter and took the bowl from her shaky hand. "Is there, girls?"

The girls giggled again as the heat rose in Lavina's cheeks. "Nope, Pa, nothing like it." Milly's voice sounded a little too satisfied to Lavina as she turned her back on the scene to gather her wits. She sliced bread on the counter and waited for a conversation to start up before she turned and placed it on the table.

"The cow kicked milk all over us," Tilly grumbled.

"The bathhouse works great, Pa," Milly said with a lilt in her voice.

Lavina stared at her food and ate while the girls chattered. Cliff had not put on another shirt, and his bare arm rubbed against Lavina while he ate. *Air, I need air.*

"Miss Lavina made a lesson plan today." Milly informed her father.

"Lessons will have to wait," he said as he pulled apart his bread and dunked it in the stew.

"Wait?" For the first time during the meal, Lavina looked him in the eye.

"I made an arrangement with my employer." He leaned towards Milly and cupped Tilly's hand. "You girls will take care of his mother while we work."

"His mother?" Lavina asked, more upset by the prospect of being left alone than she anticipated.

"She broke her ankle and needs help around the house. Nothing the girls can't handle."

Lavina could not prevent the disappointment in her tone. "Well then, I guess I will need to find something else to occupy my time," she stammered. "I will reconstruct the planner and remove art lessons and literature. Of course, your daddy is an artist, so maybe I will leave that."

Cliff shook his head. "No, you can take it out. The mill here cannot process the silver."

"Oh no," Tilly cried.

"What will you do?" Milly asked.

"I will set that dream aside for now."

"What about silverware?" Milly asked.

"I used the last of your grandmother's silverware to make your bracelets."

"Silverware?" Lavina found this statement intriguing.

"Yes, it started years ago when I broke a tine off one of my mother's forks." He smiled at the memory. "I made her the ugliest ring and bracelet out of it. She wore them to her grave."

"I have silverware!" Lavina blurted before she could stop herself.

Cliff's glare froze her words as he stood. "I wish to bathe before you go to bed if you don't mind."

Lavina felt her humiliation burn her cheeks. "No, not at all." *Why can't I learn to keep my mouth shut?*

Cliff walked into his room and grabbed a towel and a fresh shirt. "Help Lavina clean up. We need to get an early start in the morning."

"Yes, Pa." The girls jumped up and took their bowls to the sink.

"You better be in bed when I get back."

After he walked out the door Milly asked, "What will you do tomorrow, Miss Lavina?"

Lavina snapped out of her gut-kicked state of mind and popped the children's bottoms with the towel. "Oh, my darlings, don't you worry about me. I'll be here milking the cow and churning butter."

And I will send your daddy's bracelets to my godfather with a note telling him to pay in silverware.

Chapter Ten

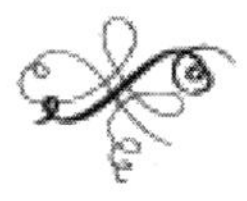

Missus Viola Glascock, who was the epitome of an old Irish emigrant, filled with joy at the sight of the girls. "You are truly blessed, Mister Walker." She winked at him as Randy's twin brother Rocky shook his hand. "I should know, mine have always been a blessing."

As the men walked to the mill, Rocky asked, "Are you the man who bought Ted Bartlett's place?"

"Yes, I purchased it for a steal." Cliff noticed the glance that passed between the brothers. "Why?"

"I hear one of Ted's marks is renting a shed from you."

Cliff eyed Rocky and asked, "Marks?"

"I believe she is number five or six. Who can keep count?" Randy laughed.

Rocky kicked a stone while they strolled. "Six, but at least this one will go home with her money. I hear Ted traveled east to meet the father of a wealthy southern girl."

"That will be a first," Randy interrupted. "Up to now, he found wealthy orphans desperate for love. If he is meeting with her father, Ted might have to marry this one."

"It sounds as if the woman staying with you might be in search of a new perspective husband." Rocky slugged Cliff's shoulder. "Lucky dog, I hear she is not only rich but quite the looker."

"I am not sure I'd want her," his brother remarked in a dubious tone. "According to David Brown at the Hub, she is mighty scary. Is that true?" Randy asked Cliff.

"She scares the hell out of me," Cliff said to end the conversation so he could sort out the information regarding Ted.

"Every mining community has bilks such as Ted. Pretending to be hardworking miners in need of capital." Randy's voice held a tinge of disgust.

As they reached the mine, Rocky grabbed up a wheelbarrow. "Ted used part of your money to buy ore samples from us."

"You didn't tell me that." Randy's voice was full of accusations.

"Where do you think the money came from to pay the doctor for fixing up Ma's leg?"

This confused Cliff. "Why did he need to buy ore samples from you? I thought he owned a mine."

"He does. It is on a poor-grade ledge," Rocky said, then handed Cliff a pick and shovel. "He needed suitable color to show his new father-in-law."

Cliff's mind reeled with confusion and anxiety for the rest of the day. On the way home, he walked in silence between the girls as they chattered about their day.

When they entered the town, the postmaster stepped out of the saloon and waved a letter in the air. "Mister Walker, Miss Lavina received a letter from the elusive Mister Bartlett." Davis glanced at the letter in his hand. "After a fashion. They sent the letter first to Georgia and then forwarded it here." He held it out to Cliff. "Can you see she gets it?"

"Can do." Cliff pocketed the tri-folded paper with its wax seal.

A few more feet down the road Milly screamed, "You can't give her that letter!"

"Hush." Cliff rushed the girls out of town beyond the stares of its occupants. "What is the matter with you?"

Milly was now in tears. "Pa, what if the letter says he ain't going to marry her?"

Cliff knelt in the dirt and held her shoulders. "What are you talking about, girl?"

Tilly hugged the back of his neck. "We don't want Lavina to go."

Milly found her voice, "She will leave. Is that what you want?"

Is that what I want? "No."

"Then you can't give her that letter."

Cliff pulled Milly to him. "It is Lavina's, and I can't keep it from her. If she leaves, we have no say in the matter."

Tilly whispered in his ear. "You can make her stay."

Cliff laughed aloud. "What would you have me do? Kidnap her?"

Milly pulled out of his embrace. "No Pa, make her fall in love with you."

Cliff unwound Tilly from his neck and stood. "She did not come here for me. She came for Ted,' he snapped and continued to walk.

"And found you. And made us fall in love with her. Now you've got to make her stay."

Cliff recognized the determination in Milly's voice and guffawed. "And just how do you suggest I do that?"

Cliff watched the cogs in Milly's brain churn. "Tell her she's pretty. Only not rude like the man in the Hub." She batted her eyes and made her voice sound dreamy. "My, you're pretty Miss Lavina."

Cliff gave a snort. "I ain't doing that."

"Well, you could do stuff for her then," Tilly begged.

He rolled his eyes and asked, "What stuff?"

"Bring her flowers, maybe," Tilly said with hesitation.

"Or make her coffee in the morning before she comes to cook breakfast." Milly's face filled with fear as she spotted Lavina heading their way. "Here she comes. Are you going to give her the letter?"

Cliff pulled the letter from his shirt and pushed it into the pocket of his pants. "I'll think on it tonight." He smiled at his tenant. "Hello, Miss Lavina."

"My, you look pretty," Milly whispered.

"How was your first day alone?"

Milly cut her eyes at him and snarled.

"Hush you," he snarled as he pushed the girls ahead of himself into the house.

The three of them froze as they stepped into the cottage. Lavina pushed past them and took in the house through their eyes. Pots and pans filled the sink, flour covered the floor, and prepared foods covered every inch of counter space.

She spun to face them. "Let me explain." She walked to the closest mound of food. "These pies and loaves of bread are for the girls to take to Missus Glascock. I am sure she misses baked goods." She pointed to the second pile of food. "I made meat pies and eclairs for you to take to work. You need to keep up your strength to swing a pick." She smiled and turned to the largest pile. "I made biscuits, butter, along with curds and whey to take to the Hub."

"The Hub? I thought you didn't care for the man there." Cliff lifted the lid from the pot on the stove.

Lavina pushed him aside to open the oven and removed its contents.

"Salt pork and beans with cornbread." She placed the bread on the table. "Yes, I have decided that if I am going to make Idaho my home, I need to mend fences."

"What are curds and whey?" Tilley asked, looking at the bowl of curdled milk.

"It's when you take good milk and make it taste horrible," Cliff grunted.

Lavina placed her hands on her hips. "Don't listen to him ladies, with salt and pepper it's delicious." Both girls looked at it and grimaced. "You will try it first before you stick your noses in the air." Lavina ladled a small portion onto their plates and added salt and pepper.

Cliff stripped off his shirt and repeated last night's ablution while the girls ate the curds with reluctance.

Lavina felt the heat rise in her cheeks and busied herself with serving the beans. As she retrieved a knife to cut the bread, Cliff placed a hand on hers. "Let me do that for you." He winked at the girls, and Lavina watched them stifle a giggle.

What are they up to now? She sat and eyed them with suspicion. When Cliff turned to place the knife on the counter, Lavina leaned toward the girls and whispered, "What are you up to Milly sly?"

Milly avoided eye contact. "You said you were going to make your home in Idaho. Does that mean you are not leaving?"

Cliff sat as Lavina leaned back in her chair. "I said if. But for my sanity and to keep you from nagging me, I promise it will not be until a month after Ted returns. It shouldn't take more than a month to see if we are compatible." The girls both clapped. "Unless of course, he sends me a letter saying he has found someone new, or we get word he has died."

Both girls looked at their father with fear. *Now I know they are up to something.*

Cliff cleared his throat. "Looks as if you've cooked enough to last the week. What will you do tomorrow?"

And he is covering for them. She stood and started the hot water in the sink. "I don't know about y'all, but I am tired of canned beef and salt pork." She scrubbed at a pan. "I plan to go hunting for an elk or deer after I drop off the food at the Hub." She then turned to face Cliff. "Will you lend me a pair of dungarees and a shirt?"

Cliff stood to retrieve the items from his room. "Here you are." When Lavina finished washing the dishes, she gathered his clothes, and left to put them in her shed.

"You can't give her that letter, Pa," the girls said in unison.

"She's going to town to take food to the Hub. What if the postmaster asks her about the letter?" Cliff tapped his fingers on the table in rapid succession. "I am going to get caught with it."

Milly touched his hand. "She won't be able to go tomorrow."

"How do you know that?"

"Because I am going to be too sick for her to go to town." She started a coughing fit.

"How is that going to help? It just puts it off a day." *Oh crap, I am in deep now.*

"No Pa, you write her a letter from Ted tonight. A romantic one telling her to please wait for you."

Cliff stood and yelled, "No girls, that's worse. That is deception." They jumped as the door to Lavina's shed slammed shut.

Both girls stared into his face. "Please, Pa. We love her. Don't let her leave."

Cliff looked at the letter he held and shoved it once more into his pocket as Lavina entered.

"I started a bath for you, Mister Walker."

"Thank you." Cliff rushed past her to his room and grabbed a towel then tucked Ted's letter under his mattress. *I can't believe I'm doing this.* He walked out the front door without another word.

Milly jumped as Lavina spun. "Give it up, girls. What is going on here?"

Tilly's mouth dropped open. "Aaaah!" she screamed then slammed her head on the table while Milly started to hack and cough.

Lavina's face filled with concern. "Do you need a drink of milk?"

"No, water." Milly coughed harder now.

"I will have to go out to the pump. Watch your sister, Tilly." Lavina grabbed the empty pail and headed out the door.

Milly smacked the back of Tilly's head which still lay on the table. "Stop that sniveling, you'll give me away." She then moved to the stove and put her forehead as close to the heat as she could, then ran back and sat at the table as Lavina reentered.

"I don't feel good," she moaned.

Lavina leaned over and kissed Milly's forehead. "You're burning up with fever!"

Milly now laid her head on the table and whimpered.

"Oh darling, you will be fine." Lavina stroked her hair. She then dipped a cloth in the cool water and laid it on Milly's head. "Tilly, you go crawl in your daddy's bed in case she is contagious. I will bring your pad and blankets and make you a bed on the floor."

As Lavina started up the ladder Milly winked at Tilly. "Pull yourself together, I got this."

Lavina doubled the girl's pad and laid it against the wall in Cliff's bedroom. "Crawl in darling." She then tucked Milly in and carried the lantern to the door. "Sweet dreams, girls," she said and pulled the door closed.

"This is going to work, Tilly. So don't ruin it." Milly's threat received another, "Aaaah!" as Tilley pulled the blanket over her head.

When Lavina turned to face the room, Cliff stood by the fire with a towel around his waist. His wet pants and shirt hung over two kitchen chairs that he pushed in front of the stove.

"Oh, my." Lavina fidgeted with her collar. *Someone get me a spoon.*

"I only have the two sets of clothes. I washed the one, and you borrowed the other."

Lavina's eyes settled on the patch of curly black hair in the middle of his chest. Droplets of water glistened in the firelight. Her tongue slid across her teeth and she swore the cool liquid rolled down her throat. "I... I put Milly on the floor by your bed just in case she needs you." Lavina hurried to the door and pulled it open. "Do not hesitate to call me if you need anything during the night." She pulled the door shut behind herself and leaned against it. *Heaven knows I won't get any sleep tonight. My word, Cliff Walters, your mamma sure can cook.*

Cliff sharpened a feather and opened a bottle of ink, then walked into his room to retrieve Ted's letter.

"What will you write, Pa?" Tilly's voice filled with fear.

"I am not sure."

Milly popped up her head. "Tell her she is pretty."

"Ted has never seen her." He walked back towards the door.

"I forgot Ted is writing to her. Don't be too nice, just nice enough to make her stay."

Cliff held up Ted's letter and said, "I think I will just reword this one." He closed the door and sat at the desk to read Ted's letter.

Dear Miss Randall,

It is with mixed feelings I am writing to you today. When I did not receive word from you after my invitation, I lost hope and headed east to find investors. As fortune has it, I met a lovely young woman whom I intend to marry. I regret any pain I may have caused you.

Respectfully, Ted Bartlett.

Cliff dipped his quill and wrote.

Dear Miss Randall,

It is with mixed feelings I write to you today. When I did not receive a reply to my invitation, I headed east to find investors. As fortune has it, I have secured capital and will head back to Atlanta, Idaho. I hope we can renew our friendship.

She is better off without him. Cliff reread the words he had written. *Is what I'm doing any better? Might as well drive the last nail in my coffin with gusto.* He shrugged and then finished the letter with a flourish.

With renewed hope in the power of love. Ted Bartlett.

Cliff tri-folded his letter, then removed Ted's letter from the outer addressed sheet of paper and reheated the dried wax. *She will never notice.* He dropped Ted's letter into the fire, where it burst into flame and withered into ash. *Too late to turn back now.*

CHAPTER ELEVEN

The delicious aromas of coffee and bacon drew Lavina out of bed, as Cliff hoped they might. "The coffee is hot," he informed her as he stirred scrambled eggs and bacon chunks.

"Thank you. What a pleasant surprise." She pinched a bite of eggs with the tips of her fingers and ate them. Lavina then sat the case she carried on the counter and poured a cup of coffee. "I brought this for you." She indicated the box. "It is Italian leather."

The box was an eleven-inch by fifteen-inch leather-covered wooden case, with contrasting leather trim and decorative brass nails.

She opened it to reveal a mirrored lid and silk lining. "I emptied it of my toiletries and thought you could use it for a lunch box." She placed in two meat pies and two eclairs she had wrapped in tissue paper from her packaged china. Next, she filled a Mason fruit jar with milk and sealed the lid. "This will suit," she said as she tucked the milk inside the box.

Cliff looked towards the bedroom door where Milly stood waving her hands and mouthing, "Say something nice."

He waved to shoo her back into the bedroom and turned to face Lavina.

He rubbed his rough, calloused hand up the smooth skin of her arm. "I wish to thank you for what you have done for me and the girls." He grinned at the shiver that ran through her body.

"Oh, my." She stepped away from his touch. "Someone must have walked on my grave." Her china dishes clanked as she set the table. "How is Milly this morning?"

On cue, Milly coughed and moaned from Cliff's bedroom. "I think it might be best if she stays with you today. If you don't mind?"

Lavina found a large crate and packed in the pies and loaves of bread she made for the Glascock family. "Not at all."

"Come and eat girls, let's get the day started." Cliff's voice raised as he ladled the eggs on their plates.

As soon as Tilly and Cliff left for work, Milly made a miraculous recovery. "All right, Milly Sly, what are you up to now?"

Milly fidgeted with the washcloth she held. "I don't have a clue what you mean."

"I won't let you get off that easy." Lavina filled the sink with water. "The sneaky goings-on last night and the sudden recovery this morning."

"I ah... I." Lavina watched as the child searched for an excuse. "I wanted to stay home with you."

Lavina pursed her lips and shook her head. "That will never do, young lady. There are things we do because they are the right thing to do. Your care of Missus Glascock makes it possible for your daddy to have a job and builds character." Shame filled Milly's face as Lavina continued. "I intended to have fun today and go hunting. But I will not reward you for your trickery."

A flash of fear came into Milly's eyes. "What are we going to do today?"

Lavina stacked the clean dishes on the counter. "I will hold Maggie while you milk her. Afterward, we will get lumber from the shed and build shelves for the kitchen." A sigh escaped Milly's lips. "And if I see you enjoying yourself, I will make you take a long, steamy bath and have a nap. As I might a genuinely sick little girl." Lavina smiled and grabbed the milk bucket. "Get a move on it, we are wasting the best part of the day."

After they milked the cow, Lavina and Milly held a board against the wall as if it were a shelf. "How do they get the shelves to stay on the wall?" There was not a single shelf in the cabin from which they might get inspiration. They set the board on two crates and stepped back. "Maybe we need to ask your daddy."

Milly pointed to the arrangement of the wood. "That looks as if it might work."

Lavina hugged her to her side. "You are a genius."

They nailed boards top and bottom to the crates on each end then attached the crates to the wall. They constructed two each for the two walls over the counters and another one over the sink.

After they finished placing the food items on the four shelves, Milly asked, "What goes above the sink?"

"Dishes. But first, let's finish out these counters by making shelves on the bottom brace boards." When they nailed the last board in, Lavina handed one of the two remaining crates to Milly and grabbed the other. "To my trunk."

Inside the shed, Lavina opened the chest and removed her remaining china, her tea set, and kitchen towels. Milly ran her hand over a lacey item. "These are pretty."

"Yes, in the South, girls start to make and collect doilies when they are your age."

"What are doilies?"

Lavina picked up the stack of linen and put it on her crate. "They make a house a home. Come, I will show you."

Inside the cabin, Lavina covered the table with a light blue linen tablecloth and pulled out her largest lace doily. It was darker blue with a white eyelet ruffle, which she placed in the center of the table.

Milly clapped. "You were right, it does make it homey in here."

Lavina then pulled out her silver tea set and said, "And we've only just begun." She sat the tray in the center. "Now find me long narrow doilies."

"I like these yellow ones," Milly said as she laid them out on the table.

"Perfect, they will give us something cheery to look at while we wash dishes." Lavina laid them on the shelves above the sink and arranged her china. "We will put your daddy's dishes under the counter with the pots and pans."

After arranging the items under the counter, Milly stood back and placed her hands on her hips. "That looks horrible."

Lavina thought for a moment. "You're right. Go into my shed. There should be a set of white sheets with little yellow flowers. Bring them and my sewing kit," she said then grabbed a knife. "I will go to the river and cut willow branches."

At the river, Lavina cut five willows and peeled the bark from them. Back in the kitchen, they stopped to make potato soup for dinner, after which Lavina cut the sheets into curtains. She made a basic fold at the top of each one and base stitched them. They slid them onto the branches and nailed them to the front of the counters and on the shelves. The last one she nailed above the window overlooking the table.

Milly turned in a circle and squealed, "It's so pretty."

Lavina sighed. "I hope your daddy doesn't get too angry with me." No sooner had she got the words out of her mouth when she heard Cliff stomping off his boots at the door. Lavina gave an involuntary cry, "Dear me." She ran to the door and slid out. "Cliff, Tilly, welcome home." She pushed Tilly through the narrow gap in the door and pulled it shut.

"Let me explain." She gave Cliff a cheesy smile. "We may have gotten a bit carried away today."

Cliff furrowed his brow. "Carried away?"

"Yes, you see. We started out with the plan to make the kitchen more convenient. And well, it may have morphed into... Well, into something you may not appreciate."

Cliff took a step towards the door she held shut and said in a condescending tone. "Let's take a look."

Lavina placed her hand on his chest and pleaded, "Please, if you're mad, can you wait until the girls are in bed to cuss me out?"

Cliff cupped her hand, and his voice now held a soothing tone. "I can do that."

Milly dragged Tilly to the far side of the table after Lavina pushed her through the door. "Listen, Pa is going to be furious."

Tilly glanced around, confused. "Why? The room is beautiful."

"Because he didn't build it or buy it."

Tilly's face flushed with fright. "Oh, no. That is true."

Milly shook her sister's shoulders. "You can't let that happen."

"Me? Why me?" Tilly pushed her sister back.

"You need to remind him that Lavina has a right to be mad at him."

"Why would she be mad at him?"

"The letter!" Milly glanced towards the opening door. "Can you do it?" Tilly jumped as the door swung open. "Can you do it?" Milly said as she pinched her.

Tilly smacked her sister's hand. "Yes, now stop that."

The girls froze as their father's face darkened when he took in the changes to his house. Lavina stood beside him with an awkward grin and her hands folded in prayer.

Milly elbowed Tilly. "Pa!" Tilly screamed and everyone stared at her in shock as she stammered, "Didn't Mister Nelson give you a letter for Miss Lavina?"

Milly's smile of relief lasted long enough to witness the glare her father threw her. "Yes." His eyes narrowed as he pulled the letter from his pocket and handed it to Lavina. "I forgot. This came for you."

Lavina took the letter from his hand and read. "It's from Ted." Milly watched with fear as she opened it and scanned her father's writing. "Bless my soul." She held it to her breast. "If you'll excuse me tonight," she said as she laid the letter on the table and buttered two slices of bread. "I will write to him tonight and take it and your package to the mail in the morning."

When she closed the door behind her, the frigid glare Cliff gave Milly caused her to slump in her chair. "She is writing to Ted." His voice was low and rattled Milly's very bones.

"I know Pa."

"And mailing it in the morning."

"I know Pa."

"Mailing it to Ted." His voice boomed.

"I know Pa. What can I do about it?" She watched her plate of beans as her head swam.

"I'm not sure, but we can't let her mail that letter."

"Lavina knows I was faking sick. I can't do it again. And Tilly could never pull off being sick." Milly felt the floor melting away beneath her.

Cliff stood, and both girls jumped as he said, "I have to tell her the truth."

In unison, they screamed, "No. Pa, please!" They ran to his side and tugged his arms.

Tilly spoke first. "She will hate us."

"And you care for her, too. I can see that you care," Milly whimpered.

Cliff knelt and met them eye to eye. "She is going to find out and the more we deceive her, the more she is going to hate us."

"She won't find out if Ted doesn't get the letter." Milly begged now, "Please Pa, I will think of something. Give me time."

He sat back on his heels. "You have until we leave in the morning. I don't want to get caught either. But I can't let her send a letter to a man who is now engaged to another."

"I will think of something, Pa," Milly promised.

They finished their dinner when Cliff stood and threw his towel over his shoulder. "You girls clean up and head to bed while I go wash off this ore dust." The girl smiled at his large, blackened hands as he waved them in their faces. "I am trusting your twisted little mind to get us out of this Milly." He then kissed her head.

"I won't let you down, Pa." She beamed.

"What will you do?" Tilly asked when their father shut the door.

"I'm not sure. But Pa trusts me, and I know he doesn't want her to leave, either. I can't let him down. We have to think of something."

"I cannot think under pressure." Tilly placed her foot on the ladder to head to bed.

"Well, that's a fine how-do-you-do!" Milly mimicked Lavina. "I cannot sleep under pressure."

CHAPTER TWELVE

As Cliff knocked on the door with his third knuckle, he asked, "Have you finished your letter?"

"Yes, I have."

He pushed the door open to the most sensual site he had ever enjoyed. Lavina laid out in the tub, clean-shaven from neck to foot, as was the custom for the rich wishing to avoid parasites. Lavina let out a blood-curdling scream, and Cliff jerked the door closed. "Sorry... I uh... Sorry."

"Pa, what's wrong?"

Cliff turned to face his girls. "Nothing. Go back in the house."

"Why did Lavina scream?" Tilly's voice filled with concern.

Milly's voice, however, was full of accusation. "You told her, didn't you?"

"No. Now get to bed." Cliff shuffled them back inside and rushed them up the ladder.

As he sat at the table, Lavina opened the door and peered inside the cabin. "Did you need something?"

Cliff jumped to his feet. "No, I… I am so sorry. I was going to bathe before I headed to bed."

Lavina pulled a chair up to the kitchen stove and unwound the towel from her damp hair. "I see. Was that everything? I thought maybe you needed to tell me something."

"Tell you something?" The girls' heads caught Cliff's eye as they popped over the rail.

"Yes. I heard the girls ask if you told me. I was wondering what they wanted you to tell me?"

Cliff cleared his throat. "I don't recall." He twisted the towel on his shoulder before he stammered, "If you don't mind, I'll go take that bath now. And again, I am sorry for walking in on you."

Lavina blushed. "And I am sorry I screamed so loud. I hope it doesn't haunt your dreams."

The corner of his mouth turned upward as he gave her a wink. "As if the vision of you in all your glory might be merciful enough to grant me sleep." As he watched the effect his words had on Lavina, the blood rushed through his veins with a notable rise in temperature. Cliff willed her to stand, then watched with amazement as she did. Two long strides brought him in front of her. He bent his head and felt the heat from her breath on his lips. As he moved closer, the whispered, "Kiss her" which escaped from Milly, broke the spell. Cliff stepped back and opened the door. "Go to bed, girls." He exited without another word.

Lavina sat on her bed in utter confusion about how Cliff's near kiss made her heart race and her head spin. Guilt filled her as she reread her simple reply to Ted's letter.

Dear Ted,

I am sorry for the confusion. The post office waylaid my last letter to you. I now reside in Atlanta, Idaho, and await your return.

Lavina Randall.

She tore the letter in two and pulled out a new piece of stationery. *I need to concentrate on Ted. This flirtation with Cliff must end.*

Dearest Ted,

I was distressed thinking about how upset you must have been, wondering if I had rejected your kind offer. The opposite is true. I wait for you in Idaho with great anticipation. I must tell you how Idaho has been an unexpected joy, I have visions of a long happy life here.

Lavina pulled a gold frame from her trunk and removed the tintype.

I am sending you this picture of myself and desire one from you. We can hold them near our hearts until at last, we meet.

Affectionately, Lavina

Milly stayed awake late into the night thinking of a plan, but failed to come up with anything. She and Tilly dressed in silence as they listened to Lavina and Cliff make breakfast. Milly watched Tilly descend the ladder with dread. *Oh, no. Pa will have to tell her.* A nail used to hold the ladder in place caught Tilly's hem and she reached up to remove it before it ripped. *Brilliant!* Milly placed her foot on the first rung of the ladder and pulled up her hem. It took two attempts to get it snagged before she slid down the ladder to the sound of tearing cloth.

Cliff ran and picked her off the floor. "Are you hurt, baby girl?"

She hugged his neck and whispered in his ear. "This is my plan." Out loud, she cried, "I tore my dress."

Cliff placed her on her feet and knelt to assess the damage. "You can't go to work in this." From the hem to the neckline was a long, jagged rip.

Lavina stroked Milly's hair. "You better wear your Sunday dress and I will help you mend this one tonight."

The girls stared at each other, open-mouthed.

Cliff stood and asked, "What is wrong?"

Tilly put her hand in his and said, "We didn't want to tell you Pa, but we cannot button them anymore."

Milly pulled her dress over her head. "Sorry Pa, we just got too big too fast."

Lavina sighed. "Well, I guess you can stay home and get your first sewing lesson."

"What of your letter to Ted?" Milly blurted.

Lavina put her hand to her forehead. "Oh yes, I forgot. Do you mind dropping it off, along with your bracelets, for me today?"

Cliff winked at Milly. "It will be my pleasure."

When Lavina left to get her mail, Milly clapped. "I told you I would think of something."

Cliff mussed her hair. "Yes, you did. I am glad this foolishness is over."

In her shed, Lavina eyed her stained dress, where she laid it over the remaining pile of lumber. *What a waste.* She ran her hand across the smooth material. *Well, it can't hurt to ask.* She peeked her head in the cabin's door. "Mister Walters, do you mind coming to my shed, so I can explain the postage on the package I need to send."

Cliff raised his eyebrows at the girls. "I guess, she doesn't think hill-folk know about postage." He followed Lavina into her shed.

"Don't be silly. I don't want to talk of postage." She picked up her dress and held it out. "This is the dress I stained. I intended to burn it. But now I was hoping, if you didn't mind, it has yards of unstained material in it. I can use it to make the girl's dresses. There might be enough for aprons as well."

Cliff touched the fabric. "I appreciate that you did not ask me in front of the girls this time, but no."

Lavina placed a hand on his arm. "You would rather I burned it?"

"No. I rather the girls did not grow unappreciative of the life I offer them." He leaned against the wall and slid one leg up the wood at a forty-five-degree angle. "I have done the best I can for my girls, and they have a good life." He rubbed a hand from thigh to knee. "They are accustomed to making do or waiting for what they need. I don't want them expecting you to come to the rescue every time they need something."

Lavina laid the dress on her bed. "I understand Mister Walters, I will just mend Milly's torn dress."

As she walked past him, he placed a hand on her shoulder and asked, "Will you burn that dress because of a stain?"

"Yes, I will. You see, they raised me..." She contemplated for a moment. "I will not say spoiled. Spoiled suggests a certain amount of love. I will say, they pampered me. It is what I am accustomed to."

"You are right. In this instance, the dress will be better served, remade and not burned." He stood tall and picked up her mail as she snatched up the dress. "But I am going to make it clear to the girls that the dresses and the work you've done, are in exchange for rent. I will not be taking your money, Miss Lavina."

Lavina gave him a sarcastic curtsy. "That suits me fine, Mister Walters. We have a deal." She turned towards the house.

"Let me make something clear to you, Miss Lavina," he added in a condescending tone. "Our agreement does not give you leave to pamper my girls."

"Oh heavens, I wouldn't dream of pampering them." A smile pulled at the corners of her mouth as she gave him a sideways glance.

"I see." He snorted. "So, we are clear on the subject. I don't want you spoiling them either."

As soon as Cliff and Tilly left the house, he sensed the child was ready to burst. "Do you have something to say to me, Tilly?"

Tilly pulled her hair out of her mouth that she sucked on out of habit. "Why didn't you kiss Miss Lavina last night?"

Cliff placed a hand on her head. "Are you now plotting with Milly?"

"No, I just want to see you happy, and I believe Lavina will make us happy."

Cliff furrowed his brow. "Are we unhappy?"

"Not unhappy, just not whole happy."

Since his mother's death, Cliff was aware of just how much the girls missed having a woman around the place. "So, you and Milly figure I need your plots and plans to get a woman?"

"Well, yes."

"I'm not as helpless as you think. I won your mother's heart."

"Yes, but you were young then."

Cliff roared with laughter. "I am not that old, but I am experienced. I have to ask myself why a rich, beautiful woman such as Lavina, came hundreds of miles into the wilderness to marry a man she doesn't know."

"And what answer did you find?"

"It wasn't to escape prejudice, as she claims," he explained. "Her uncle moved to New York, a city they say, that never sleeps. Lavina could have family, parties, and men falling at her feet."

"That sounds exciting."

"Yes, any young woman might think so." He winked at Tilly. "I assume Lavina wanted a quiet life away from that world and she figured Ted was the only means to that end. Last night I planted a seed that needs time to sprout. I must be careful not to drown it out."

After pulling the seams out of her stained dress, the bodice produced three yards of material. Another five yards from the underskirt, eight yards of foundation skirt and bustle, and five yards of material from the apron overskirt, which Lavina set to one side. "That part is stained, but we can make y'all pinafores to keep your new dresses from getting dirty."

She then disassembled the girl's church dresses. With the added material, Lavina fashioned two simple dresses with pinafores and bonnets as well as two new church dresses. She set the pattern pieces aside and started their dinner. "I will have to work on the dresses tomorrow. For now, we will mend your old dress and if I work fast tonight, I can have the pinafores finished by morning."

"I thought you were going to make yourself work clothes." Milly fingered the brocade of the dress.

"I was, and I will, but since I am not standing around with only my underdrawers to wear. I will do yours first."

"You are always talking about not wasting things, but this seems a silly waste of material just to make you have a goose bottom." Milly's grin widened.

"Oh, you." Lavina lunged out and bear-hugged her. "Hush your mouth, or I am going to give you a goose bottom." She pushed her away and slapped the child's hind end.

"Pa likes your goose bottom."

Lavina's mouth dropped open. "Oh hush, he said no such thing."

"He didn't need to say it. I just know because he is always staring at it." Milly bugged out her eyes in imitation of her father. "Like you did when you were admiring his belt buckle." She stretched out the word admiring, then giggled. "You must admire the hair on his chest and his back pockets too." She held her ribs and laughed aloud.

Lavina felt the flood of blood in her cheeks and pushed Milly out the door. "Go catch Maggie before I tie a knot in your tail."

"You remind me of the girl with the red coat, in the story our grandma used to tell us." Milly continued to tease her as she walked away. "My, what big eyes you have, Mister Walters."

Oh, that child is too observant for my liking. All the more reason to curb my contact with Cliff.

Chapter Thirteen

Tilly's disappointment that there was no new dress showed on her face. "Tomorrow night, Tilly Shy, I promise," Lavina said.

"Come and look at them." Milly pulled Tilly to the pile of pattern pieces.

Cliff followed, then reached out to touch. Milly pushed his hand away. "Don't get them dirty, Pa."

"Sorry, I will wash up first." As he rolled up his sleeves and washed his arms, Lavina watched the girls out of the corner of her eye.

Milly whispered into Tilly's ear, and Tilly pulled back and shook her head. Milly grabbed her shoulders and whispered again. *What are they up to now?* Milly pushed her sister toward their father. "Do it," she whispered and nodded.

Tilly shrugged. "My Pa, what big muscles you have."

Milly burst into laughter when Lavina's jaw dropped open. *You rat fink.* She turned to hide her flushed cheeks.

Cliff did not miss a beat. He scooped Tilly up and held her tight. "The better to squeeze you with, my dear."

Lavina sewed late into the night to finish the pinafores, and by the next night, she had their plain dresses and bonnets complete. by Sunday she could dress the girls in their church clothes. "But there is no church here," Milly pointed out.

"I am aware of that, but we can still have food, fellowship, and celebrate the Lord. I made a pie and bread. I will go with you girls today to Missus Glascock's home and we can all enjoy the Lord's day, together."

It thrilled Misses Glascock to have a female visitor. "Call me Ivy, dear."

Lavina made coffee and served the pie. "I have not had a chance to meet anyone in town besides the postmaster, the proprietor at the market, and the man at the Hub. Are there many women in Atlanta?"

"A few, but they too, are busy in the mines while the ground is workable. The big mines can operate year-round because they have the equipment and men. The rest of us all need to pitch in where we can. I don't know what we might have done had your man and girls not come our way."

Lavina blushed. "They are not my girls, and Mister Walker is not my man."

"That should be easily remedied for a pretty girl such as yourself."

Lavina watched the girls' smiles and had an overwhelming desire to run. "I have a man, or will, once Ted Bartlett comes home."

"Yes, Ted doesn't sound a very sensible man," Ivy said in her blunt manner. "Leaving just when the season started. You best hope he gets enough capital to survive the winter."

Lavina was desperate to change the tone of this conversation. "How long does the season last?" she asked as she poured them more coffee.

"Anywhere from three to five months, depending on the weather. Winters are long here, and so much work needs to go into preparing for them."

"Such as?" The idea that people needed to prepare for winter had never occurred to Lavina.

"Food for man and beast and wood for the fire."

How can Cliff put up enough feed for the stock if he works in the mine all summer? He owned two horses, a milk cow, four beef cows, and a bull. *I have some planning to do, but first I must seek information.*

"The men flock to these places and only realize the value of a good hard-working woman after they've been here a while." Missus Glascock patted Lavina's hand. "Cliff is lucky you came into his life when you did."

Lavina glanced down at her hands. "As I said before, I did not come into Mister Walker's life. I am here for Ted Bartlett."

Missus Glascock's disapproval showed on her face. "Well, I don't really know your Cliff and I have only heard rumors of Mister Bartlett. But if you want my advice. Don't go throwing away a good man in search of the dream of a better one. In my experience, young women's dreams are silly and not worth the pillow she dreamed them on."

Lavina's mouth dropped open. "I am uncertain how I should take that," she stammered.

"I am just saying, if I were you, I might concentrate on the unwrapped gifts before me. I wouldn't concern myself with the brown paper package coming in the mail." Missus Glascock looked at the twins and said, "Girls, I was wondering if you would go dig up strawberry plants for Miss Lavina. There is a crate on the porch you can put them in it."

"Yes ma'am." The girls jumped up and ran out into the garden.

"Thank you," Lavina said, surprised at the turn the conversation took.

"I was just getting them out of the house." She picked up Lavina's hand and patted it. "I admit a black man would not be my first choice either, but perhaps you come from more open-minded people."

Lavina's hackles rose. "As a matter of fact, I do come from open-minded people. But as I said before, I did not come for Cliff." Lavina reiterated as she stood.

"Sit down child." Ivy pulled her back into the chair. "All I am saying is, if you have no family to object and no personal issue with the color of his skin. You might want to keep your mind open about your prospects."

"My prospects?"

"Yes, Cliff here saw an opportunity to have a share in a mine without laying out any money. He saw our need and his own and did not hesitate to make it benefit both of us."

The girls opened the door and stared at Lavina while Missus Glascock continued her tirade.

"While Ted, on the other hand, did not have the forethought to find investors during the winter months. Now he will not see a profit from his mine for an entire year."

Lavina pulled her hand back and stood. "I must leave, girls. I need to stop at the market on my way home." She gathered her gloves and satchel. "I will get dinner ready for when y'all get back."

Missus Glascock reached out, grabbed her hand, and pleaded. "It will be a long winter for these girls and their Pa, without the aid of a good woman. You think on that whilst you dream of Ted."

"I will consider your advice." Lavina could not prevent the snark from entering her tone. Nor could she shake Missus Glascock's assessment of her life choices, or of the winter Cliff and his girls might suffer without help. *As if my catholic guilt needed fuel.*

The walk to town produced a jumble of thoughts and worries. Lavina set aside the comments concerning Cliff and herself to concentrate on the more immediate needs of the family.

In Georgia, the farmers used horse-drawn reapers, which replaced scythes after the Civil War. Lavina was certain if she could get ahold of one, she might be able to put up enough feed for winter. *Now how do I convince Cliff to let me purchase one?*

Lavina stopped at the market where Davis Nelson sat in a chair reading his newspaper. "I wonder, can I get a subscription to that paper?" Lavina asked.

Davis held up the paper. The front-page headline read: *The Country Mourns.* It was an article concerning the assassination of President Lincoln.

"That was five years ago."

Davis smiled as he folded and laid it in his lap. "Yes, I know, but it is the only paper in town."

"He has read it a thousand times." Carl laughed. "How can I help you today, Miss Randall?"

"I noticed you have a couple of dresses stuffed behind the mining equipment."

"Those were from Ted's first..." Davis smacked Carl in the chest with his paper which caused him to stop speaking.

Lavina eyed them with suspicion. "Ted's, what?"

Davis spoke first, "Ted's idea."

"That's right." Carl gave a rapid nod of his head. "Ted thought, if we carried women's clothing, women would soon follow." Davis threw an arm around Carl's shoulder as they grinned and nodded.

"Stop that. You look like a couple of idiots. I don't give two figs for what Ted plotted. Just fetch them for me, please." It was too soon after Missus Glascock's assessments of Ted, to hear more recounting of Ted's failings from these two.

Carl worked his way through the equipment and shook the dust off the dresses. "Here you are."

Lavina touched the material. "They are dreadfully thin."

"Yes, miss, that is the style out here. Plus, at that point, the girl had run out of," Carl stopped speaking as Davis shook his head. "Time! Yeah, she ran out of time and didn't add more layers and frills and such."

"I don't have the time or patience to figure out what kind of game y'all are playing." Lavina snatched the dresses from his hand. "I'll take them, and I need potatoes, onions, salt, and some of your canned beef."

"You'll be relieved to know a butcher is setting up shop down the road." Davis offered to ease the tension.

Lavina huffed. "Well, that is something, I guess." The two buffoons had stepped on her last nerve. "I was also wondering if you possess or if you can get ahold of a Hussie Reaper?"

"I have a farm implement catalog you can order from." Carl pulled the book out from under the counter. "Don't get much call for farm equipment in a mining town."

Lavina found a sickle-bar mower for $75.

"Would you like me to order it for you?"

"I will need to talk to Mister Walters first," she said as she closed the catalog.

"Not Ted Bartlett?" Davis raised a brow and pursed his lips.

"Ted is a mine owner, not a plowboy. However, Cliff owns livestock and will need to put up feed for the winter." She gathered her supplies and paid Carl. Neither man said another word, but Lavina felt her ears burning as she walked home. *Pish, what do I care what they think?*

At dinner that night, Lavina again asked to borrow Cliff's clothes. "I saw elk sign today. Maggie was at the furthest end of the place and there appeared to be elk beds up the draw."

"Why was Maggie that far away?" Cliff asked as he retrieved his pants and a shirt from the bedroom.

"I assume she is closer to calving than you believe. She acts mighty uncomfortable."

Cliff stood to light a lantern and walked out the door. A half-hour later, he was back. "You are right. Enjoy the last of the milk for a couple of weeks, girls."

"Why Pa?" Tilly asked.

"Maggie needs to build up colostrum for the new calf or else it will die."

Milly perked up. "At least we won't need to eat curds and whey for a while."

"Shush your mouth," Lavina tried to sound indignant, then addressed Cliff. "I made your lunch for tomorrow. If you and the girls can see to breakfast, I want to be in a position to kill an elk before first light."

Cliff did not look up and spoke in a voice devoid of emotion. "Good luck on your hunt."

Lavina watched as the girls frowned at their father. Milly hit his arm and rolled her eyes while Cliff shrugged his shoulders. *What is she up to now?*

"Pa was telling us on the way home today how nice it was to come home to a clean house and a hot meal," Milly commented as she elbowed her sister.

"That's right, and how half of his worries left, with you here," Tilly added. "He only has to concern himself with work and not fret over the animals or home."

Cliff stared open-mouthed at both his girls, then winked at Lavina. "And how the sun shines brighter, and everything tastes like bacon." They both laughed until tears formed in their eyes while the girls pouted. Cliff placed his dish in the sink and then went to retrieve his towel from the bedroom. As he opened the door, he addressed Lavina again. "But seriously, the clouds blew away when you arrived, and life became sunshine and rainbows."

Lavina, who was now at the sink washing dishes, splashed water at him. "Yes, yes, and the birds sang louder, and the grass grew greener. Go take your bath."

When the door closed, Lavina's lips held a slight smile as she let out a long sigh. "Humm."

"Are you happy, Miss Lavina?" Tilly asked.

For a long moment, Lavina stared into the child's face then answered, "Very much so, my love."

CHAPTER FOURTEEN

Cliff had coffee on the stove well before dawn, and the eggs cooked when Lavina entered.

"Thank you." She poured herself a cup and laid an envelope on the counter. "Will you drop this by the post office today?"

Cliff took the envelope and read the address. *For all that is holy, will this never end?* "Did you receive another letter from Ted?"

"No." Lavina ate her eggs. "I have questions I need to be answered."

He sat across from her and tapped the letter on the table. "I imagine you do."

Lavina's head snapped. "What is that supposed to mean?"

"I just meant I would have hundreds of questions to ask before I married a total stranger." He watched the anger on her face and pushed her further. "Of course, I am guessing I might have asked them before I traveled a thousand miles into the wilderness."

Lavina threw back the last of her coffee and slammed the cup on the table. "For your information, Mister Walters, I asked questions, but new ones come up as my state of affairs changes." She grabbed her gun and walked out the door without saying goodbye.

Cliff walked to the window and watched her walk across the field. When she was out of sight, he put water in her teapot and set it on the stove. After the steam broke the seal on her envelope, he read the words, noting she did not fill this one with the same romantic air as her prior letter.

Ted,

I need to get something clear in my mind. I am happy to wait here for your return as long as I understand the arrangement between us. If marriage is no longer your desire, I fear I must move on with my life.

I await your reply, Lavina.

Oh, damn. Cliff pulled out a fresh piece of paper and a quill. *I cannot believe I'm going to do this.*

Dearest Lavina,

It relieved me to receive your letter. So much so, I found the first jeweler and bought a wedding ring. Please wait for my return.

Yours truly, Ted

As Cliff and the girls headed to town, he asked Milly, "Do you think you can do something sneaky for me today?"

Milly laughed. "Oh, Pa. If you only knew the truth of the matter."

"I am sure I do not want to know the truth." He mussed her hair. "I need you to stamp this letter with Mister Nelson's stamp at the post office while I distract him."

Milly grabbed Cliff's hand. "Did you write Miss Lavina another letter?"

"Yes, I did."

"But why, Pa?"

Tilly spoke on his behalf. "He is planting seeds."

"What does that mean?" Milly asked, confused.

Cliff remained silent to see if Tilly understood what he had meant. She did. "He is planting love seeds and watching them grow."

The thick aroma of stinging nettle filled Lavina's nostrils and reminded her to use caution as she worked her way up the riverbank. It was the last week in May and calves were on the ground. The bulls grew new antlers, and Lavina hoped to find a young one to shoot.

She climbed the hill on the opposite side of the draw from where she saw the beds yesterday. As she sat in silence and waited for the sun to rise, Lavina gained a new sense of self. After a lifetime of purposelessness, this was a welcome change. *There is something in these mountains I was not aware of calling to me.*

When the rays of sunlight hit the deep draw, Lavina listened to the call of the cows to their calves as they wrestled from their grass beds. A huge bull elk stood. His antlers were small velvet clumps, and Lavina assumed he had injured them while sparring. She pulled her rifle to her shoulder, took careful aim, and squeezed the trigger.

As her target crumpled in the grass, the herd exploded and ran in unison up the mountain. Lavina watched while bulls and cows worked to protect the calves as they disappeared over the horizon. *Oh, goodness. That was magnificent.*

The beat of her heart filled her ears as she slit the animal's throat to let its blood drain. The bull was not as big as she expected. *But I still have plenty of work.*

She found a two-foot branch to spread the hind legs while she removed its guts. When she had it in place, she froze in shock. Her bull elk, with its wonky antlers, had female genitalia. *What in the world? I hope the meat is edible.*

When she finished gutting the animal, Lavina headed home with its heart and liver. She placed them in two bowls and found an ax. Back outside, she caught Cliff's horse and found a length of rope.

It took Lavina the rest of the morning to quarter up the elk, tie it onto the horse, and work her way back home. Her lunch comprised bread and butter and the last of her curds. She then used the horse to hoist the meat into the branches of a tree in front of the cabin. After which she led the horse to a grove of alder, where she tied two fallen logs to him and led him home.

Back at his pasture, she ran her hands through his thick mane. "Thank you, boy. I wish I had grain for you." In the cabin, Lavina started a dinner of fried heart, baked potatoes, and some wild asparagus she had found at the alder grove.

"I cooked up the liver with onions for your lunch and the girls can take the rest to Missus Glascock tomorrow."

"When I tried to drop off your letter this morning, there was one for you." He handed her both letters. "I kept yours in case Ted's letter answered your questions."

Lavina ripped open Ted's letter and read. "Yes, it does," she said as she opened the firebox of the stove and tossed in the letter she had written.

Cliff nodded his head toward the window. "That is an impressive amount of meat."

"I was afraid it might not be good to eat. But the heart tastes fine."

Cliff wrinkled his forehead. "Why would it not be fit to eat?"

"It was the strangest thing. The elk had antlers, but it was a cow."

Cliff raised his brows. "I have heard of female deer and elk getting so old that they grew antlers. They say the antlers never fall off and stay in the velvet stage."

"Do you think the meat is safe?"

"I don't know why it wouldn't be. I guess if we end up sharing a toilet seat tonight, we will find out."

Tilly grimaced. "I don't want to eat it."

"Yeah, Pa. I'll just eat a potato." Milly chimed.

"Good." Lavina winked at the girls. "Leaves more heart for me and your daddy."

Cliff took a bite of meat. "Mmm, oh Miss Lavina, that is the best thing I ate this entire year."

"Yes, and I just love heart." Lavina licked her fingers.

Both girls grabbed a piece and ate with gusto. "Oh Pa, heart is delicious. I don't even care if we get the runs."

Lavina winked at Cliff. "Well, girls, I will be your roommate for a few days." They jumped up and hugged her neck.

"Roommate?" Cliff ate an asparagus spear. "Oh, dang, that's good too."

Lavina smiled with pride. "Thank you. And yes, the bathhouse will make the perfect smokehouse. If you move my trunk and cot in here, I will dig a fire pit under the drain. I can make an arched oven with rocks and the drain will serve as a chimney, drawing the smoke into the bathhouse. If I lay willow sticks over the bath, I could put the meat on them, and it should smoke up nice."

"That sounds like a big job. Do you want one of the girls to stay and help?"

"No, I can manage."

"Missus Glascock was right." Cliff smiled at the girls while Lavina's blood boiled at the mention of the old woman's name.

What has that old coot been filling their heads with, I wonder? Lavina could not forget the woman's intrusion into her affairs. *I am not responsible for the Walters family's happiness just because I showed up on their doorstep.* "And about what is Missus Glascock right?"

"She told the girls and me we underappreciated the value of a good, robust woman." Cliff put an arm around Lavina and shook an asparagus tip under her nose. "She said if we had any brains at all, we would never let you leave."

Lavina shrugged his arm off and stood. "Well, she is smarter than I gave her credit." Lavina put her plate in the sink. "After tonight, you must walk home past the falls to bathe."

Cliff followed her to the sink, leaned over her shoulder, and sniffed her hair. "You are pretty ripe after everything you've done today. I'll let you bathe first tonight."

As his breath tickled her ear, she folded her arms across her breast. *Do not let him get the best of you tonight. Throw it back at him.* "No, you go first. This time I'll check to see if you have finished."

Cliff threw his head back as his laughter shook the rafters. "I'll be sure to leave the door unlocked."

Lavina covered her flaming hot cheeks as Tilly asked, "What's wrong, Miss Lavina?"

"Nothing." She slapped Cliff's chest with her wet washcloth. "Come, my loves, let's clean up and get to bed."

Once they had both bathed Lavina sat in front of the fire and unwound the towel from her hair. "I have given some thought to what you said this morning, and I am inclined to believe you are right."

Cliff leaned forward in his chair and asked, "Concerning what?"

"I should have asked more questions of Ted before I left Georgia. I got the impression from the gentlemen at the general store everything may not be on the up and up concerning Ted." She ran her fingers through her hair. "It leads me to conclude that I should inquire of Ted from the people he lived and worked with, day in and day out."

Cliff leaned back in his chair and crossed his legs. "Are you sure you want to make a conclusion of the man from rumors and innuendos?"

"You are right. I best not attempt it. I had to live down plenty of things I did not do in grade school." Her smile turned into deep lines on her forehead. "The simplest way would be to contact the women, but the ads I found produced neither name nor address." Lavina looked at the desk that sat beside Cliff. "When you purchased this house, did you bring that desk, or was it here already?"

Cliff entwined his fingers and rested his elbows on the arms of his chair. "It was here. The house came furnished other than our beds."

Lavina wrinkled her brow at his trembling hands. "Was the writing pad in it, or is that yours as well?"

"It was in the desk." Cliff's knuckles turned white. "What are you getting at?"

Lavina stood and walked to the desk. "Have you used the pad?"

"Um, no."

Lavina could not discern why he acted so nervous. "I wonder if I could lift his writing from the paper."

"Why might you do that?"

"It may have more answers than I have at present."

Cliff wiped a drop of sweat from his brow. "How do you intend to lift them?"

"By making a rub with one of my chalk pastels." She headed for the door and said, "I will be right back."

Moments later, she entered with a pastel and sat at the desk. As she ran the chalk over the paper, her name appeared in various forms with hearts and flowers. Lavina Randall, Miss Lavina Randall, Missus Lavina Bartlett. The heat in her cheek rose as she tore the paper out and tossed it in the fire before Cliff could see the words written on it.

"Did you find any answers?"

"Yes, I believe I did." She smiled and glided to the door. "Good night, Mister Walters."

After the door to Lavina's shed closed, Cliff stood and stretched the tension out of his shoulders. He pulled three sheets of paper from inside his shirt. Two were blank, and the other had Lavina Randall, Miss Lavina Randall, Missus Lavina Bartlett, written in his bold hand. He laid the pencil back on the desk and tossed the papers on the fire.

CHAPTER FIFTEEN

Ted's teenage girl scribbles on the pad put Lavina's mind at ease somewhat. But no amount of arduous work could keep red flags from popping up in her mind. As she smoked and canned the last of the meat, the comments and innuendos of her acquaintances at the market nagged at her. The glances between Rocky and Randy during her visit to the Glascock's home told her that Ted was not what he portrayed himself to be in his letters.

She tried three times this week to write him a letter, only to find her mind empty of anything but accusations towards him and guilt for her own behavior. *It's not as if I can write and tell him I spend my days thinking of things to discuss with Cliff.*

It relieved Lavina that the girls were not at home during the day. Her thoughts of Cliff kept her in a perpetual state of blush, while reliving their conversations, caused her to laugh out loud. *They would think me crazy.*

Did she dare to tell Ted how she grabbed Cliff's firm, round buttocks to prevent him from falling as he removed the smoked hocks that hung from her ceiling? *It took two days for my hand to stop tingling.*

Should she mention how at least once a day Cliff found a way to breathe in her ear? Which produced the annoying effect of making her nipples harden. Lavina now had an arsenal of inventive, if not ridiculous, ways of hiding them afterward. The thin cotton dresses she purchased, and the lack of corset, made them more noticeable.

I might mention that the sound of the girls' laughter causes my ovaries to ache. Will Ted be interested to learn of their strange new twin talk whenever she blushed over something Cliff said or did?

Milly and Tilly giggled about planting seeds and watching them grow. They giggled over how she was a sprout, or that she was leafing out. They even commented to their father on how she needed more water or sunlight. All of which brought a smile to Cliff's lips and made her feel the butt end of a long-running joke.

Today she felt determined to move her cot back into the shed. It had been two days since Cliff took the last of the meat out, and the constant state of euphoria from his every touch, look, and outright flirtation was more than she could bear. Lavina sat at the table with her lunch and a fresh sheet of stationery.

I need to start an emotional and spiritual relationship with Ted. It was neither her nor Ted's fault that the girls stole her heart at first sight. That her spirit connected to them on every level. But most of all the emotional bond that developed because of their shared motherless raising. What was she to do as to the physical effects of Cliff? And now, with her overwhelming concern for the girls and the homestead?

The fact she and the Walkers had fallen into a family-style routine was the result of Ted's absence. *I will draw him into my life and experiences here and bond with him in a spiritual way.* Lavina vowed to only give her time and attention to the Walkers. *I will reserve my mind and soul for my correspondence with Ted.*

For an hour she stared at the blank sheet of paper while empty, dried-out, incoherent thoughts ran through her mind. *Pish, get on with it.*

Dear Ted,

The days have grown long. This country is so beautiful and is fast becoming a part of me. I cannot imagine sleeping to the sound of a busy street again. I have never in my life experienced peace, so soul-cleansing as listening to the rocks roll in the river, the rustle of the leaves in the Aspen trees, or the chatter of the chipmunks as they roam the forest floor. I saw a Brook trout in the river today and wished I knew how to fish. Fresh fish would be a treat.

I envision our walks together, and it lightens the weight in my heart. I imagine conversations we might have, the goals we might set, and the dreams we might accomplish together. These things make my time here, without you, bearable.

Awaiting your return, Lavina

She decided not to walk to town and mail the letter, she would assign the job to Cliff. *This should stop him from whispering in my ear once he sees I am in an active relationship with Ted. Well, of sorts.*

Cliff stuck Lavina's letter in his pocket and read it during his lunch break. On the way home, he told the girls a story of fishing with his mother as a boy. "Can you take us fishing, Pa?" Tilly asked.

I knew I could count on you, Tilly girl. "We don't have any fishing equipment," Cliff explained.

"Does it cost a great deal of money?" Milly's voice filled with disappointment.

"I have a nickel, that might buy line and hooks. You can make poles out of willow sticks like your grandma and I used to do."

"Oh, thank you Pa," they cried in unison as he gave them the nickel.

"There is a package for Miss Lavina," Davis informed Cliff as they entered the mercantile. "It's small but heavy. I will go grab it for you."

The package bore an address from a jeweler in Georgia. "Thank you."

As they approached the house, Lavina ran out to greet them. The girls shook the bag of fishing tackle. "Look what Pa got us."

Lavina bent and said in a shaky voice, "Yes, yes. Not now girls. Go into the house, I need to smooth something over with your daddy." The girls' eyes bugged as Cliff frowned.

"You have a package," he said as the girl slithered into the house.

Lavina grabbed it. "Oh, it couldn't have come at a better time. It is for you."

"For me?"

"I had my godfather pay you in silverware. During the war, people sold him bits of their services. I told him that those broken forks and knives he kept would be pay enough for your bracelets." She hefted the box. "Look how heavy. Open it up and see."

Cliff took the box and tried to push past her. "I will, once we get inside the house."

"I rather you did now. Then once we go inside, you can remember what I did for you and not strangle me."

Cliff raised an eyebrow. "What have you done now?"

She shook her head and stammered, "I cannot explain what came over me today. I told the girls I'd let them help me paint my shed. But then I got bored and wanted to just brighten up the fireplace a bit. And Well the project took on a mind of its own and..."

Cliff sidestepped her and walked inside the cabin.

"Pa, isn't it beautiful?" Milly asked from the fireplace.

On one side was a giant tree. A limb of the tree went across the mantle and on the other side she had painted Cliff as he pushed the girls on a swing that hung from the limb. *Good night can the woman not just sit still*? The girl's faces pleaded with him. "Yes, it is very pretty. Miss Lavina is quite the artist."

"Your daddy's face tells me his genuine feelings." Lavina laughed then said, "But I am going to take the compliment. Now come girls, what did you have to show me?"

The girls squealed and poured their sack of tackle on the table. "We asked Pa to teach us how to fish. Do you want to learn to fish?" Milly asked.

Lavina sat at the table and fingered a hook as she squinted at Cliff. "Strange, I was just thinking that last night."

Cliff leaned over the back of her chair and picked up the line while he spoke into her ear. "Tomorrow is Saturday. If you make us willow poles, I will teach you how to fish on Sunday."

A knowing smile crossed his lips as Lavina tucked a tea towel in her collar and stood to serve dinner. Milly whispered to Tilly. "That should make her bloom."

Lavina put down their plates, then sat at the table and rapped her fingers on it while Cliff sorted through the silverware. "Ladies, we are going to have to have a discussion on social mores."

Both girls hung their heads. "What are social... what did she call them?" Tilly asked.

Milly shrugged her shoulders. "More rays?"

"Mores are things society deems proper or inappropriate, acceptable or unacceptable. Now I don't know about Montana but in Georgia, if one constantly makes another person the butt end of a private joke while in public, we consider this rude."

Both girls played with their dresses under the table. "Sorry, Miss Lavina," they said in unison.

"Now I don't know, but this talk of seeds and blooming. It needs to stop."

"It will miss Lavina. We promise," Tilly said.

Milly smiled and elbowed her sister, then placed her hand on her heart. Tilly followed suit. "I swear," they said again in unison.

"I am going to take you at your word and speak no more of this. Now come help me serve dinner."

At the river the next morning, Lavina cut four six-foot willows and stripped them clean. She had seen fishing poles before and knew they needed round eyes to put the line through and a real to wrap it around at the bottom. *A real is mechanical and I have little knowledge of mechanics. But I do have an idea for the eyes.* Lavina dug in her sewing kit and found her stash of hooks and eyes she used as replacements on her corset.

She made three tiny notches in the willow and sewed on the eyes as tight as possible, then weaved in the line. *That works.* She laid her creation on the table while she put her chin in her hands to envision how they could wind up the line. *I got it.*

Lavina picked up a hook and opened its latch wider with her knife. She then sewed two of them, three inches apart, facing each other. *It needs a groove around the bottom.* When she finished carving the groove, Lavina tied the line inside of it, then wound as much as she could around the two hooks. She cut the line and attached a hook and sinker. *Let's see how you work.*

Outside, Lavina unwound the line from the hook and made her first cast. The sinker took it out the full fifteen feet. She then wound it back. *Perfect.*

When she completed the other four poles, she baked bread and started a roast for dinner. *This way we can have sliced roast elk sandwiches on our fishing trip.*

The sound of the girls chattering as they approached the cabin made Lavina clap. *My girls are home.* She froze as a flood of guilt and realization flooded her mind. *You are not here for them.*

"I told Rocky and Randy I was spending the day with my family," Cliff announced as he stomped the ore from his boots.

Lavina cut the bread and placed it on the table. "Were they upset?"

Cliff leaned over her shoulder and pinched a piece of bread. "Mmm," he said in her ear. "Nothing like the smell of fresh bread." She pushed past him to pull the roast from the oven as he continued. "No, they said it will give them time to bring in more wood for the winter."

"I drug up more wood today when I cut the willows for our poles."

"Oh, where are they?" Tilly and Milly cried in unison.

Lavina pointed with the ladle she used to scoop the potatoes onto the tray. "Behind the door."

The three Walters ran to see them. Cliff inspected it. "This is genius, Lavina. Thank you."

Lavina ignored the girls' raised eyebrows and snickered 'seeds' comment, more disturbed over his use of her name. *He always calls me Miss. What can this mean?*

Chapter Sixteen

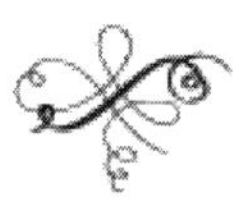

Today is the day. The day the Walkers and I celebrate a family day. And how am I supposed to keep from being emotionally and spiritually detached? Good question.

The highs and lows Lavina experienced made her volatile. The bonds formed with every moment she spent with Cliff and his girls, pushed aside the wish to bond with Ted.

Lavina packed their picnic lunch with a mixture of delight and grief. Delight at the opportunity to learn to fish and to play with the girls. Grief at the knowledge that this might close the lid on the casket of her and Ted's faux relationship.

They saturated the stroll to the river with giggles and conversations about their plans for harvest time and when they might gather wood. Cliff talked of his dreams, of what he might make from the silverware, and how grateful he was to her. The girls picked flowers to weave in her hair, and life was perfect. *Now to prevent my guilt from overtaking my joy.*

Her fishing poles worked fine, only the fish were not interested in the game. Tilly and Milly soon grew bored waiting for a fish to bite and stripped to their underclothes to jump in a pool downstream. The sun beat with no mercy on them, and Cliff had removed his shirt earlier. Lavina took off her shoes and stockings and dangled her feet in the river. "If you were not here, I could join the girls."

Cliff sauntered to where she sat to stretch out beside her on the grass and winked. "Why not? I couldn't possibly see more than I have already."

Lavina gave him a light slap. "Oh, hush your mouth." She then examined her handprint on his shoulder and exclaimed, "Your skin is turning purple."

Cliff glanced over his shoulder and shrugged. "It's getting sunburnt."

Lavina peered closer. "Sunburnt? I had no idea you... Uh..." Her voice trailed.

"That black people sunburned?"

Heat rushed to her cheeks. "Well, excuse me for being raised in a world where people didn't give a second thought to Blacks." She jumped to her feet. "Girls!" she screamed. "Come here now."

Milly and Tilly scrambled up the bank and ran to where they sat. "What's wrong, Miss Lavina?" Milly asked.

Tilly's face filled with fright. "Did you see another bear?"

"No," Lavina said as she examined their skin. "Oh, dear. Come with me." She took their hands and led them to a grove of Aspen trees. Cliff followed.

"In the south, white mammas are a bit neurotic. They slather their girls in buttermilk, make them cover every inch of their lily-white skin, and carry parasols." She knelt in front of the first tree and rubbed her hands on the bark. "Because the sun is not our friend. It makes your skin blotchy and turns it to leather as you get old." She showed them her hands covered in white powder. "I read a beauty tip article from *Godey's Lady's Book.* It told how Native Americans use the powder from Aspen trees to block the sun." Lavina applied it to both their faces.

"Get more and cover your arms and legs. The article also said bear grease will help after you burn your skin. If I ever see our bear again, we'll save the grease and see how well it works. I imagine it might make your skin as soft as a baby's bottom." She applied more powder to the back of the girls' necks.

"I imagine." Cliff's voice sounded dubious. "It makes you smell of old boots too."

"Oh, shush you." Lavina rubbed her hands on another tree. "Kneel here and let me cover your shoulders and back."

As she put the powder on his back, she watched the girls smile at each other and mouth the words 'seeds.' She dusted off her hands and snapped, "Seeds, seeds, seeds. What is with you two? Now let's eat lunch and no more talk of seeds, or I'm going to plant seeds myself."

The girls skipped away, hand in hand. "You just did." They giggled.

Cliff shrugged his shoulders and followed them.

I do not understand this running joke.

Cliff laid out a blanket and Lavina passed out roast elk sandwiches and water. "At home on a sweltering day such as this, I would serve lemonade. But alas, our grocer does not carry any lemons."

"Randy told me that his family makes a run into Boise before winter for any supplies they need. If you are still with us in September, we can take the wagon. I am sure they carry a wider variety there."

"I was curious if that was the case. When I asked Carl about putting in a garden, he told me the season was too short for most everything except perennials."

"Our farm in Montana wasn't this high in elevation, and we had a hard go of making a garden most years."

"A greenhouse is what we need." Lavina's suggestion raised everyone's brow. "It is a frame house with nothing but windows for walls. It gathers the sun's heat during the day and keeps it most of the night. It provides months more growth at each end of the season."

"Did you own one?" Tilly asked.

Lavina laughed. "Bless your heart, no. But I saw plenty."

"I thought Georgia was hot." Milly took a drink and waited for an answer.

"It is, dear."

"Then why did they need a greenhouse?"

"Well, we do experience hazardous weather in the south and have a short winter. But people use greenhouses to protect their prize plants or to enjoy greens the entire year."

The girls became bored with the conversation and finished their sandwiches in a rush. "Can we go back to our swimming hole?"

"For a short time." Cliff explained, "Lavina wants help to move back into her shed today."

Lavina watched the girls' faces fall. "It's not as if I'm moving across town," she assured them before they ran and jumped back into the water.

Cliff stretched out and put his hands behind his head to lie flat. "I think I've had enough waiting on fish for one day."

"I don't know much when it comes to fish, but maybe it was too warm today." Lavina stretched out on her stomach in the opposite direction then folded her arms to lay her head in the crook. "When will you set up your forge?"

"That will need to wait for winter." He covered his eyes. "But I do appreciate what you did for me."

"And now you have my godfather's address, and I am sure he can sell whatever you send his way." Lavina yawned and closed her eyes.

The twins awoke them an hour later by dripping water on their heads. "Ready to go home now?" Tilly asked.

"We are as wrinkly as Missus Glascock," Milly said in her thick southern drawl she had been using the entire day.

Lavina sat up and used her mother's tone. "I need to talk with you girls."

The girls cut their eyes at each other and then sat on the blanket next to her. "Bless your heart," Milly said.

"One, in the south, bless your heart is not a compliment." Lavina moved the girls around in front of her. "Two, imitation is the greatest form of flattery, and I am flattered. However." Lavina looked Milly in the eye. "I enjoy Milly and Tilly. A confident lady does not need to imitate anyone. Nor does she need to put on airs or change herself to suit others."

Milly hung her head.

"Listen." Lavina pushed up her chin. "This is a hard world for a woman, but if she stays true to herself, she can make it." Lavina smiled at them. "Now this doesn't mean you can treat people nasty then use the excuse that nasty is who you are, and you are staying true to yourself. We are children of God, and he has called us to become Christ-like."

She stared into the girls' faces and softened her look. "A strong, intelligent, Christian woman will always gain the respect of her peers." Lavina hesitated for a moment. *They need to hear it from someone, it should be someone who loves them.*

She tucked them into her sides and continued. "Listen, you will endure more than most. Unfortunately, we live in a very ignorant world and people are going to say and do cruel things for no other reason than the color of your skin. At those times, I want you to be so secure in who you are that their ignorance won't make you fall apart or doubt your true value and place in this world."

"Lavina," Tilly whispered.

"Yes, my love?"

"If God made us in his image, why do we have different colors of skin?"

Lavina kissed her head. "Because our souls are the image of God, which he breathed into man." She released the girls and placed the remains of lunch back in Cliff's box. "I want you to always remember that. Our souls are the same. They make us family. Man's ignorance does not change that. I thought I could escape prejudice when I came out West. I now know escape is impossible, so you must learn to face it head-on. Only those secure in who they are can do this."

"Lavina," Milly spoke in her normal voice now.

"Yes, Milly?"

"I won't imitate you anymore, but I hope I grow up to be just like you."

Lavina's voice caught in her throat as tears filled her eyes.

"Grab the poles, girls and let's head home." Cliff stood and pulled Lavina to her feet as the girls gathered the fishing equipment. He shook out the blanket and laid it over her arm, then placed his lunch box handle in her hand while Lavina stood frozen. The love she bore his girls hit her with a tidal wave of force and she could not shake her desire to call them her own.

Cliff leaned in and placed a warm kiss on her cheek. "Thank you for everything you do for my girls," he whispered in her ear. He then walked a few feet, picked a log off the ground, and placed it on his shoulders. The girls ran ahead, unaffected by the day, while Lavina still did not move. "Lavina?" She touched her cheek where Cliff kissed it and stared at the giant. "Are you coming home with us?"

Lavina forced her feet to work, even if her voice could not. *Home, I am going home.* She made dinner in a trance-like state while Cliff and the girls moved her belongings back into her shed. The disembodied euphoria that enveloped her mind at the river would not release its grip.

What am I doing? She lost all memory of the conversation during dinner. *Did I say a word? Did they talk? What am I doing?*

"Lavina?" Cliff's voice penetrated her stodgy thoughts.

"Yes. I'm sorry. What did you say?" She stared into the confused faces of the entire Walker family.

"The girls said goodnight."

"They're going to bed before we clean?"

Cliff furrowed his brow as Lavina glanced around to see that they had cleared the table, swept the floor, and washed the dishes. A half-drunk cup of coffee sat in front of her. She stared at it in shock as Cliff reached out and cupped her hand. "Are you alright?"

Lavina pulled her hand back and jumped to her feet. "No! No, I had too much sun today." She kissed the girls on their heads. "I think I will go lie down, as well." She then kissed the top of Cliff's head. "Goodnight, sweet dreams." Lavina walked out the door to the open-mouth stares of the entire Walker family.

During the night, she sat straight up in bed and lit a lantern, then pulled out her stationery and wrote.

Dear Ted,

My life here has become everything I could wish for myself. The mountains called to me in tones of welcome. The river roars out a song that makes my soul dance. The howl of the coyote and hoot of the owl speak to me in a language that soothes my worried mind and assures me I am not alone. I will always be grateful to you for this opportunity. Being here has made me realize what is truly valuable and what my heart will always aspire to attain.

Lavina

CHAPTER SEVENTEEN

Lavina laid her letter next to Cliff's coffee cup and started cooking breakfast.

"More questions you need to be answered?" Cliff asked as he pocketed the letter.

"No, just thoughts I wanted to share with Ted."

Will this never end? I guess I need to ramp up my game. "I don't suppose you care to share them with me?"

"I don't suppose I do."

Cliff recognized the determination Lavina used to keep him at a distance. "Then do you mind if I share something with you?"

Lavina placed their plates on the table and sat. "Please do. I would love for you to share your thoughts."

"Yesterday, out fishing with my girls, I realized how much I have been missing my mother and the girls. There is a lot to be said for working for yourself." He saw Lavina listened with intent and continued. "I came here with a dream. I thought silver would line the streets and miners would be willing to give it to me." He took a sip of coffee. "Now I trade my back and family life for a bit of coin."

Lavina's eyes softened, and he recognized the opportunity before him. "Dreams do not always manifest in the way you expect them to sometimes, Lavina. You need to be open to them becoming something new." He took her hand in his. "My mother used to say if you place your life in God's hands, he will take you where you need to be. The hardship and disappointment on the journey are there so you can appreciate what you have when you get to where he meant you to be."

Lavina pulled her hand away. "Your mother sounds to be a clever woman."

"She was. But what amazed me most was how she never got bitter." He finished his eggs. "She used to say I was her greatest blessing in life, who came into a world that was incapable of appreciating her choice. She did not let their ignorance define her truth. She said their opinions would not change the greeting she received at the pearly gates."

"That is beautiful."

Cliff noticed a tear on Lavina's cheek as he continued, "There was only ever one man's opinion my mother cared for, and he died on a cross. Be willing to walk the path God has laid before you. If your dream has become something you no longer recognize, look for God's hand in it, then make your final decisions wisely."

Make my decision wisely? It's a little too late for that. I made my decision months ago. I will not let heat and passion prevent me from keeping my

word.

Lavina understood that she and Ted were not engaged, but they had made promises. She was positive her attraction to Cliff was physical because of their proximity and his lack of competition. It was her ever-growing love for the girls she struggled with most. *How will I ever walk away and leave them?*

But she felt she owed it to Ted to wait for his return when she could then make a careful, well-thought-through decision. Determined not to let the physical take control of her mental reasoning, Lavina made an alternative plan. *Demanding work and physical distance are what I need.*

She spent the day gathering wood and piling it behind the house. Lavina did not know how much wood it might take to last the winter but had decided no matter how much she hauled, it would not be enough.

Maggie became more uncomfortable by the moment, and there were visible signs of springing and mucus. *It will not be long now, old girl.* Lavina never saw so much as the birth of a kitten and hoped it did not happen while she was alone. *I will be lost if she has problems.*

The day passed as days of hard labor often do. She had little time to think about her problems, and before she knew it, the girls and Cliff were home.

"Lavina, you do not need to gather wood. I can get it in the fall," Cliff said as she greeted them.

"You're welcome."

"I'm sorry, thank you, Lavina." He smiled and kissed her cheek. "I just meant you do not have to work this hard."

The heck I don't. Lavina touched the warmth his kiss left on her flesh and said, "You will need to put up feed for the winter. I was just clearing out the fields for more growth and easier reaping."

As they entered the house, she grinned at the disappointment on Cliff's face. She had placed their dinner on the table to avoid the pre-meal shenanigans at the counter.

Irritation crossed his brow as he pulled out her chair. "I think I will sell all but the milk cow and horses to the new butcher in town." He then sat and took a bite of the elk steak. "With such delicious meat available, it seems pointless to keep them."

"Will they bring enough money to buy a horse-drawn sickle bar mower?"

"Not hardly," Cliff blustered. "I will be lucky to get $50 out of them. My scythe will have to do. Besides, I need to wait until March when they calve out and that will be too late for your plan."

Not a word. Keep your mouth shut. Don't insult him by offering to buy it. "I forgot to tell you, but it looks as if Maggie will calve any minute."

Cliff jumped up and walked out the door without shutting it, and was back in moments. "You're right. I will have to check on her during the night."

"Oh Pa, we want to be there when the baby is born," Tilly cried.

"Wake us up, please Pa," Milly begged then turned to Lavina. "Don't you want to see the baby be born?"

"I would love that. I have seen nothing born before."

Tilly wrinkled her nose. "Most of the birth is pretty awful, but then the baby is so cute, and you forget the other stuff."

"I just hope no problems arise, and she has it by herself.," Cliff said as he sat to finish his dinner.

Lavina's mind filled with concern. "What do you do if a problem occurs?"

"That's when Pa wraps a rope around the front feet and pulls it out." Milly informed her. "Otherwise, she'll die like our Ma did."

A devastating silence filled the room. *Goodness Cliff, say something, anything.* When Lavina realized he could not talk, she said the only thing that came to her mind. "We will have to make sure that does not happen."

Tilly hugged her father's arm. "Yeah, 'cause the baby doesn't have a good Pa to take care of it like we do."

Lavina reached out and pulled Milly to her side. "True. Few people are as lucky as you girls to have such a wonderful daddy."

Milly threw her arms around Lavina's neck and wailed, "I'm sorry. I forgot you had no Ma or Pa."

"Oh my love, I did not mean it that way." Her voice caught in her throat. "I am sorry your Mamma died."

Tilly ran to hug Lavina. "Yes, but you had no one, and we had Pa, and now we have you."

Another thick silence filled the room as fear grew in the three Walters' faces. "I meant..." Tilly stammered as she sucked in a strand of hair.

Lavina pulled the hair out of her mouth and said, "I understood what you meant. I love you too." Lavina needed to change the suffocating temperature of the conversation. "Now let's wash the dishes and get to bed, in case your daddy has to wake us up for the birth."

And how are you going to leave these girls behind?

After waking the girls for the expected event, Cliff knocked on Lavina's door. "She is having the calf."

Lavina opened the door and pulled on her dressing gown. "Is she having problems?"

"No, so we need to be quiet and stand back." The four of them walked to the fence and squatted in the grass. "Don't scare her or she will jump up and may not lay down again for hours."

They sat in silence as the cow pushed and panted, groaned, and bellowed. Cliff whispered in Lavina's ear and pointed. "If the pads of the hoof point toward the ground, everything should be fine, unless the calf is too big. If the pads are ever pointing up, it means the calf is breech and everything is a mess." He inhaled the fragrance of her hair as a vision of a permanent life together filled his mind. *Tell her the truth before it is too late. Before she hates you for it.*

"What do you do then?"

"If the cow doesn't have the calf pushed too far out, you can try to push it back in and turn it around right." His explanation caused her to grimace. "It's difficult and you have to make sure it does not turn his head back. You do it by what you can feel with your hand inside her."

"I had no idea ranching could be so gruesome."

"I told you it was," Tilly said.

"Tell her about the time you had to cut a calf in two to get it out, Pa," Milly said with a rather morbid delight.

Cliff shook his head when he saw Lavina turn pale. "I am sure she does not want me to tell that story."

Lavina swallowed hard. "Yes, let's save that story for another day."

"Are you going to be sick?" Milly giggled.

"Hush up, I am a city girl, we don't stick our hands in cows'... hinnies." She blushed then squealed, "Here comes the nose."

"It won't be long now," Milly said.

The cow gave one long push, and the calf came out midway. As she stood, the calf flopped onto the ground with a thud. "Oh, dear!" Lavina screamed.

Cliff stood and helped her to her feet. "It's fine, it happens."

The mother started to lick the sack off its head and Lavina asked, "What is that?"

"The placenta, the bag the calf was inside of the womb. The sack is filled with water and serves as a barrier to protect and nourish the calf." Cliff noted her face filled with questions.

Lavina tugged at his shirt and pulled his ear to her mouth. "Is that the same for every animal?"

"Yes." Cliff chuckled. "Even humans."

Lavina pursed her lips and swallowed twice. "I see, thank you."

The girls walked along the fence to get a closer look at the calf. When a coyote howled, they ran back. "Do you hear that, Pa?" Milly asked.

Tilly pulled on his hand. "I'm scared. Let's go back in the house."

Cliff eyed Lavina's reaction and smiled. "Nothing to be afraid of, Tilly Girl. I find great peace in the howls and hoots of the night. Let's a body feel they're not alone in the world."

"I don't like it." Tilly tugged harder. "Do you Miss Lavina?"

"Yes." Cliff noted the hesitation in her voice. "Your daddy's right," she said as she gave Cliff a pensive look. "It soothes the soul." She bobbed her head goodnight and walked in silence back to the shed.

Cliff sent the girls into the house, then stopped Lavina and asked, "How was your first birth experience?"

Lavina rubbed her finger under her nose. "It was very enlightening."

"The other cows won't calve out for a while. Do you think you could handle a birth if you were here by yourself?"

Fear flashed in her eyes. "I suppose. I will try my best."

Cliff took her hand and kissed the back of it. "That is what I love about you, Lavina. You are game for new experiences." The blush that covered her face brought a smile to his lips. "Good night, sweet dreams."

"Sweet night, I mean good dreams." She fanned the air with her hand. "Glory be, I mean good night, Mister Walker."

Cliff tucked his thumbs into the top of his jeans and sauntered back to the cabin. *Yeah, she is hooked. Now time to reel her in.*

CHAPTER EIGHTEEN

Summer was now in full swing, and Lavina spent the week in search of berries and wild greens. The watercress went over well, as did the asparagus and wild onions. She transported the roots of the asparagus to the side of the cabin along with rhubarb from Carl Burks and strawberries from Missus Glascock. She was back to milking the cow to keep the calf from having milk scours, and her days were full and lonesome.

The days grew longer, which meant Cliff could work longer, which meant she was alone longer. She stained two more dresses and made four more for the girls in ascending sizes. She will not bother to ask their father for permission to give them to the girls. *I will just leave them in the shed when I go. He can do what he likes with them after that.*

Lavina spent the morning in the garden and prepared to transplant the chamomile she found, as the girls yelled at her. "This was our last day of work." Milly's voice filled with excitement.

Oh Hallelujah! Lavina stood and dusted off her hands and knees. "How fortuitous." She walked with them into the house. "The currant berries are ripe, and I could use the extra hands."

Tilly scrunched up her face. "Currant berries?"

"Yes, we will make jams and syrup for the winter and a pie as a reward for your aid." The girls clapped and squealed. "And if we find enough, I will make tarts for your daddy's lunch."

"Sounds delicious. I hope you find plenty," Cliff said as he sliced the roast.

"First, we will walk into town tomorrow for sugar, jars, and green apples."

Tilly placed the bread on the table. "What will we do with the green apples?"

"They have pectin in them. That is the ingredient that makes jams and jellies bind."

"There is a chokecherry tree by the Hot Springs, and if you crawl into the thick brush by the river, you'll find a wild cherry tree. There are plum trees that we pass on the way to work as well." Cliff informed her.

"Oh, girls, we will have a full larder. Now if only we had a larder." She smiled and poured two cups of coffee. "I saw wild strawberries and blackberries while hunting, but it looks as if they produce more pain than pleasure."

"There will be elderberries and huckleberries later," Cliff said as he ate.

"Elderberries!" She winked at Cliff. "I can make wine and cordial for the long winter."

He leaned into her ear and whispered, "Are you trying to ply me with liquor? That could be fun."

My word. Lavina's mouth dropped as she shoved him back and fanned her face. "Is it hot in here?" She walked to the door and stepped out to the sound of the girls' giggles. Her predicament with Cliff had not dissipated, nor did her lack of anything to communicate to Ted, that held any value.

The only truths she had reached were her love for Milly and Tilly, and her growing attraction to Cliff. She wasn't even certain why she bothered fighting the truth. *Because you gave your word.*

The next morning Lavina yelled, "Dress in your Sunday clothes today, girls." She had put on one of her elaborate bustle dresses this morning and wore an apron to cook their breakfast.

"Why?" the girls asked in unison from the loft.

"We don't go to town every day and a lady should always look her best in public."

Cliff sipped his coffee and said, "I will check the plums today to see if they are ripe."

"I hope they are not. We will have plenty to do with the currants this week."

"There are jars under the girls' bed. Not many, but enough to get you started." Cliff stood and grabbed his lunch box. "I will pay you back for the supplies when I get paid if you want to keep a running account of the cost."

Keep your mouth closed and agree. "I will, if that is what you desire."

Cliff leaned over her shoulder as she scrambled the girls' eggs and whispered, "That's one of my desires." He left before Lavina could find her voice.

Cliff heard enough about Ted Bartlett to ease his conscience. *She deserves a good man, and he is not an honest one from what everyone has to say.*

Randy was more than eager to elaborate on the underhanded dealings of Ted. "That first girl was little more than a child, and her father soon lost his property holdings in the war. Ted sent her back with a broken heart and a vast experience of men."

"Vast?" Cliff let his mouth drop open.

"Yes, she was so desperate to stay she agreed to whore herself out for him to sustain his habits."

"Habits?"

"Oh, Ted likes his whiskey and cards."

"He sounds like a real piece of work."

"The next three women were much older." Randy's laughter wrang of cynicism. "And wiser. Wise enough to figure out Ted's game, they all left within a week."

"What of the last two women?" Cliff asked.

Rocky and Randy cut their eyes at each other as Randy said. "One of them could have fed a family of five for the winter. He kept her around just long enough to spend her fortune."

"And the other?"

"And the other was a very confused young man." The Glascock boys burst into laughter. "You should have seen the look on Ted's face when his fiancé stepped out of the stagecoach in a bustle and a beard." Rocky slapped Cliff's shoulder. "I would pay good money to watch that again."

I might be a louse for deceiving Lavina, but I am better than this lowlife, womanizing, scoundrel.

Lavina rubbed the heat from Cliff's breath off her cheek. *I must learn to avoid his whispers and stop him from invading my personal space.*

"We are ready." Milly's voice made Lavina jump.

"Come, girls, we are off to town." Lavina grabbed her satchel and opened the door. The Mercantile possessed fifty canning jars in the storage area.

"Not much call for them in a mining town," Carl informed Lavina as he ordered her one hundred and fifty more.

"Planning to stay the winter, I see," Davis Nelson said as he flipped down his paper.

Lavina cast a smirk his way. "Regardless. No use wasting the good fruit available." She closed the gap between them. "There have been no letters for me?"

"No, ma'am, not since the last one." He winked at Carl. "Ted might have his hands full."

Lavina cut her eyes at the proprietor, who squelched a smile and jumped. "With investors and such," he said, as a blush covered his face.

It appears I am the butt end of everybody's jokes. Lavina handed Tilly two ten-pound bags of sugar, then gave a crate of apples to Milly, both of whom looked to be bursting to say something.

Bless your hearts, I don't want to listen to you today. Lavina paid for two peppermint sticks and stuck them in the girls' mouths, then picked up the crates of jars." Davis scurried to open the door. "Thank you, gentlemen, good day."

The girls' arms became tired and Lavina did not get to enjoy the silent trip home she wished for. They stopped three times to rest, and each time their peppermint sticks popped out and their mouths popped open.

"Are you sad Ted didn't write?"

"You won't leave, will you?"

"Maybe Mister Nelson is right, and Ted is too busy."

"Or maybe they sent your letter to the wrong place again."

"Or men don't think as women do and Ted doesn't understand it makes you sad."

"You shouldn't worry. I bet he writes to you any day."

Lavina rushed the girls into the cabin. "It is too hot to pick berries. Let's get set up for canning and storage."

"What can we do to help?" Milly asked.

"First you girls get the jars from under your bed. You will need to wash and boil them. I will build another shelf under the counter for storage."

The girls had not run out of questions, as Lavina hoped. Their interest took a more personal note. "Why don't you like Pa?" Tilly asked.

"What makes you think that?" Lavina intended to avoid actual answers.

"Because you want Ted to write to you." Tilly pouted.

"Wanting to receive a letter from Ted does not mean I don't care for your daddy." Lavina continued to hammer, which was the only interim in the girls' obsessive interrogation of her.

"Would you like Pa more if he spoke more?" Milly asked.

"He talks plenty." Lavina placed another board as Milly asked her fatal question, which demanded an answer.

"Is it because he is black?"

The board fell from Lavina's grasp. "Hush your mouth!" She took both girls by the hand and sat them at the table. "I understand your concern, we do live in a world that frowns on mixed marriages." She poured herself a fresh cup of coffee. *This is going to be a hard conversation to have.*

She sat back down at the table. "Not only is it a tragedy for the couple in love, but a loss for humanity. If your momma and grandma had not disregarded what the world thinks, you might not be here. And that my loves would be a terrible loss."

Now how do I answer the question without answering the question?

Lavina reached across and stroked the girls' cheeks. "My people raised me to see the souls of humans, not the color of their skin. When I look at your father, well, first I see a giant." The girls smiled. "But then I see a good man who works hard and loves the Lord. A man with great tenderness for his children. Who opened his home to a stranger and has shown great patience. A man any woman might be proud to marry."

Tilly sucked on a strand of hair. "But you like Ted more?"

Lavina rubbed her temples and sighed. "I don't know Ted that well. But I made him a promise to wait until he returns to decide whether I will marry him."

"Oh." Realization dawned on Milly's face. "I hope he is short and lazy and a heathen who gets easily irritated."

"And hates children," Tilly added.

For the rest of the day, the girls' self-drawn conclusions that Ted could never measure up to their father appeared to satisfy them.

When Cliff entered his home, Lavina and the girls were putting the last nail into the new shelves. He reached out a hand to help Lavina off the floor, only to have her ignore it and stand on her own. Cliff followed her to where she stirred the stew. He intended to whisper 'mmm good' into her ear, only to have her turn and push the hot ladle to his lips. "Try this."

He sampled it and in the sultriest voice he could muster, whispered, "Divine."

"Dinner is ready!" Lavina screamed, causing everyone in the room to jump.

What game is she playing?

The table was rectangular, and two chairs had been set on either side since Lavina arrived. Cliff and she normally sat opposite the girls. Tonight, Lavina arranged for the chairs to sit on all four sides of the table. "This is the customary way to arrange a table," Lavina told the girls. "The adults at the head and foot with the children in the middle."

Cliff leaned towards her to say 'as one big happy family' but Lavina sidestepped him to leave his words hanging in the air.

She is quicker than I gave her credit for.

Cliff had stopped washing in the sink once they finished the bathhouse and limited his activity to washing his hands before dinner. Tonight, he pulled off his shirt and hung it by the door. "I hope you don't mind, but it was hot today, and I don't want my aroma to ruin our dinner." He then washed in the sink with slow, deliberate movements and watched as Lavina blushed throughout their shirtless meal.

That's right, sweetheart, two can play at this game.

Chapter Nineteen

The moment Lavina left the house, the girls descended the ladder and started in on Cliff. "You need to write Lavina another letter," Milly said.

"Yes, Pa, she doesn't love Ted. She is waiting to find out if he is better than you."

Cliff raised his brows. "Is that what she told you?"

"Well, not quite, but that's what she meant."

Milly sat beside him. "So, we were thinking if you wrote her a letter from Ted and said things like, you hated work and God."

Tilly interrupted, "And kids, don't forget to make him hate kids."

"And how everybody irritates you and you hate waiting for people to give you money."

"Oh, and ask her for money," Tilly added.

Cliff hit his fist on the table. "No, that is not going to happen. I should have never let you talk me into this in the first place. The deception ends here."

"But Pa, what if she marries him and leaves?"

Cliff pulled the girls to him. "Then she leaves, but I don't suppose she will."

"But Pa."

"That is enough girls." He pulled them around to stand in front of him and knelt. "I don't want Lavina to stay because she considers me better than Ted. Nor do I want her to stay because she considered this her only option." He pulled Tilly's hair out of her mouth. "I want her to stay for the same reason we want her to stay."

Tilly pulled a strand of hair across her lips. "Why do we want her to stay?"

Milly slapped her hand away from her mouth. "Because we love her, dummy."

Cliff held both girls' hands. "That's right, and don't call your sister a dummy."

Tilly used her other hand to wrap a strand of hair around and around as Cliff watched her use great restraint not to suck on it. "How are we going to make her fall in love with us?"

"She's already in love with us, dum... It's Pa, who needs to make her fall in love with him."

Tilly slid into his chest. "Do you think you can do it?"

"I believe I have. Now I need her to admit it." *Her attempts to avoid me today tell their own story.* Cliff kissed the girls on their cheeks. "Now go back to bed."

Cliff waited an hour for Lavina's customary return to dry her hair in front of the fire before he peered out the window. He did not see her light under the door. *I understand how she intends to play. We will find out who has a better grasp of the game of love.*

Over the next few days, Cliff made it clear to Lavina how small the house was. He had no intention of chasing her around, and being the giant he was, it only took a well-placed sidestep to have her run into him.

"Bless my soul, I did not see you there." Lavina bounced off his chest for the third time tonight. "I don't know what's gotten into me."

Cliff held onto her shoulders to help keep her balanced while he pulled her in close. "I might question your eyesight, but I am too big to miss. I'm beginning to wonder if you are doing it intentionally." He gave a slight smirk as she twisted to turn her back to him. He then leaned over to whisper in her ear, "Don't worry, intentional or not, I rather enjoy you bumping into me." He turned and walked to the shed with his towel.

Cliff missed their nightly talks without the girls. As he stepped out of the tub, his foot came in contact with a pipe wrench. Lavina had mentioned she used it to tighten the pipe because of a small leak.

He peeked out the door and saw Lavina at the stove as she removed the last of the canning jars from the boiling water. *Let's find out if she can avoid me tonight.* Cliff dressed and stepped back into the drained tub to loosen the pipe until a spray of water shot into the air. It made a direct line to Lavina's cot.

He saw Lavina preparing to escape as he entered. *Think quick.* At the mine, a falling rock had hit him in the lower back as he bent over, which left a small abrasion and bruise. He blocked her exit. "I was wondering if you might look at something?"

Lavina drew out the word, yes, as she eyed him with caution.

"Nothing weird, just a scratch. I am afraid I may have infected it." He lifted his shirt and turned his back to her.

Lavina leaned in close and touched the skin surrounding the scratch. "It is a little red but doesn't appear infected. I can wrap it before you leave for work tomorrow if you wish."

He pulled his shirt down as he turned towards her and spoke in a smoky voice. "Hum, wrap me up then."

Lavina's cheeks flushed red as she pushed past him out the door.

One, two, three, four, five.

"Oh no! Cliff, come quick!

Right on cue. Cliff ran inside the shed and looked around the room with feigned panic. "Where did you put the wrench?"

Lavina now searched the room like a lunatic as water sprayed over both of them. She tossed bedding and clothes in the air, then fell on her knees and swiped under the cot. "I found it!"

Cliff tightened the spigot as he sat on the edge of the tub. "Well, you can't sleep in here tonight." He looked up and observed tears in Lavina's eyes. "Come now, it's not the end of the world." He grabbed her entire cot. "Everything will dry out."

Lavina held the doors open for him as he carried her cot into the main house. He hung his wet shirt on its customary nail before they started to hang her linen. They covered the chairs, tables, counters, and even his desk. He placed her cot in front of the fireplace and noticed Lavina shiver. "Go take off those wet clothes and wrap up in my blanket. I will bring in your trunk and we can get it dried out along with your other belongings."

While he was out, Lavina draped the clothes she wore over the cot and tucked his blanket around her naked body. When he returned, he laid out her clothes from the trunk.

"Well, I guess I have no secrets now," she said as he shook out her pantaloons and stockings.

"You have plenty of secrets I wish to hear."

Lavina stared at him wide-eyed. "Such as?"

"Such as, what are you hoping for in life? What are your dreams, what are your plans?"

"I have to confess, as a woman of means, I never gave it much consideration." She snatched her nightgown from his hand and hung it in front of the fire.

"You must have dreamed of your new life as you travel to Idaho," he said as he continued to hang her other garments.

"It is silly."

"I want to hear it all the same." Cliff now stood beside her to dry the pants he wore.

"I had the schoolgirl notion that I could look into someone's heart and find my reflection there."

Cliff stared into her eyes for a long moment. "And you thought you might find that in the heart of a man you've never met?" He held Lavina's eyes captive with sheer willpower.

"Stranger things have happened."

"You don't have to tell me. I am a staunch believer in love at first sight."

Lavina dropped her gaze to the floor. "My nightgown is dry now. I guess I will head up to bed."

What is the matter with me? Lavina's efforts to keep Cliff at a distance had produced the opposite effect. *Every time I try to prevent him from getting close, I end up bumping into him.* She even sat on his lap, not realizing he occupied the chair she vacated.

As she started to climb the ladder to sleep with the girls, Cliff pushed open the door to his room. "You can sleep in my bed." He said in his husky tone.

The heat rose in her cheeks as she stared into his face. He smiled and pushed a strand of loose hair behind her ear. "I will sleep upstairs."

Lavina knew they both felt her tremble at his touch. Embarrassed, she stepped off the ladder onto his foot. "Ouch." Her head jerked up as Cliff looked down, causing their heads to collide. "Damn girl."

"Sorry. Oh, sorry." She rubbed her forehead and gave a nervous giggle.

Cliff mussed her hair with his enormous paw. "Go to bed Lavina, you're tired."

She ducked under his arm into his room as she stammered, "Goodnight Cliff." Lavina shut the door and leaned against it in the dark. *What is wrong with me?* She reprimanded herself. *You almost said yes when you thought he was talking about sleeping with him.* Her entire body flushed with heat. *Pull it together, girl, you've lost your mind.*

She pulled her nightgown on and crawled into Cliff's warm bed while she inhaled the manly aroma of his sheets. *Oh, Lavina child, at least be honest with yourself. You haven't lost your mind; you've lost your heart.*

It took two days for her shed and belongings to dry out, even after she made a clothesline and hung them in the sun. It was a make-shift line, but today she intended to make a permanent one.

Milly, who sensed the tension between her father and Lavina, was eager to please her today. She ran out and dug two holes fifteen feet apart while Tilly and Lavina drug up two eight-foot logs. Milly had made the holes two feet deep and gathered small rocks to secure the bases.

After they placed the logs in the holes, Lavina held them straight while Milly and Tilly stomped in the rocks and dirt. "They need to be good and solid, girls," Lavina said.

Milly grabbed her shovel and turned it upside-down to tamp in the base. "That should work."

Lavina tried to jiggle the post, but it did not budge. "Perfect."

"How are we going to attach the cross board?" Tilly asked.

Lavina found two two-by-fours four feet long behind her shed. "I believe we can tie a rope to each end of the crossbeam." She rolled a stump of wood to the post. "I will slide the beam into place, then you girls will pull the ropes tight to hold it there while I hammer it onto the post."

"Sounds good," Milly said as she and her sister walked to the ends of the ropes. "Okay Tilly, when she says go, lean into the rope like a mule pulling a cart."

Once Lavina had her balance on the stump, she slid the board in place and yelled, "Ready when you are."

Both girls placed the ropes over their shoulders and pulled forward as hard as they could. The dried-out lumber snapped in two and sent the twins flat on their faces. Milly giggled. "We are two tough old mules."

Tilly sat up and screamed, "Miss Lavina, Miss Lavina."

Lavina lay stretched out flat on her back, knocked out cold. When the girls reached her side, Tilly fainted at the sight of the blood that streamed from Lavina's head. The board had hit Lavina in the temple, splitting the skin from the top of her forehead to above her ear.

Milly ran to the house and fetched a pail of water and a towel. When she came back, Tilly woke and cried, "What happened?"

"She is hurt bad. You need to go get Pa."

Tilly looked around in fright. "What if I meet a bear?"

"Fine!" Milly flopped beside Lavina's head and soaked the towel in the cool water. She placed it on the cut while she took Tilly's hand and put it on top. "Press hard and don't let her get up if she comes to. I will go get Pa."

"I can't," Tilly whimpered.

"Well, I can't do both. Do you want her to bleed to death before I get back?"

Tilly held the towel tight against Lavina's scalp. "No. I can do it."

Milly ran the entire way to the mine. "Pa!" she screamed from the entrance with what little air she could muster. "Pa, come quick."

The three men dropped their picks and ran out to find Milly with blood-covered hands. Cliff fell to his knees and grabbed her shoulders.

"What happened?" he screamed.

Milly panted and sputtered, "She is hurt bad, Pa." She held her ribs and tried to catch her breath. "Tilly," she panted. "Tilly," she huffed out again.

Cliff shook her. "Is she dead?"

"No. She is with Lavina," she panted as Cliff's patience wore thin.

"Spit it out, child," he snapped.

"Lavina's head is cut open and she won't wake up."

Cliff jumped up and ran. "Make sure she gets home safe," he yelled over his shoulder.

Chapter Twenty

As Cliff ran through town, he made a detour to the Hub. "I need a bottle of whiskey." He threw two bits on the counter and snatched the bottle from the barkeeper.

Tilly rushed to him when he got close enough to see them. "Pa, she is awake now, but you need to sew her head. I can see the bone." He hurried to Lavina's side, scooped her off the ground, and carried her into the kitchen. "Grab your grandmother's kit out of my room, baby girl." He set Lavina on a chair and found a coffee cup. "You need to drink," he said as he filled it with whiskey.

Lavina pulled the towel from her head. "Has it stopped bleeding?"

Cliff examined the wound. "It has slowed, keep the pressure on it, and drink." He pushed the cup to her lips.

Lavina took a sip and coughed. "That burns."

"Not as much as sewing you up is going to if you don't drink it."

Lavina forced it down as Tilly came back with the medical kit.

"I am guessing you use a razor," Cliff said as he pulled out the thread and a curved needle. "I will need it."

Lavina blushed. "For what?"

"I am sorry, but I will need to shave back the hair." Lavina's face turned pale. "I promise it won't be much, but it needs doing."

Lavina looked at Tilly. "It is in my trunk, wrapped in white canvas."

While Tilly ran to get it, Cliff filled Lavina's cup once more. "Drink." He then stripped off his shirt and washed his upper torso and hands.

Milly thundered through the door. "Is she going to be ok?"

"Yes, baby girl. Did Rocky and Randy come with you?"

"No, I took off right after you. Your fast, Pa."

Milly held Lavina's hand. "How do you feel?"

"Like I don't have lips." She strummed her lower lip. "Psh, psh, psh."

Milly's face filled with fright. "What is wrong with her, Pa?"

"She is enjoying the effects of the whiskey."

Tilly burst through the door. "I found it, Pa." She held up the razor.

"Why do you use a razor?" Milly asked. "Women don't have beards."

Lavina giggled. "It helps keep creepy crawlies out of your crevices."

Tilly and Milly stared at her. "Your what?"

Lavina burst out in laughter. "Your..."

"Girls," Cliff yelled, which made them jump. "Why don't you go outside while I do this? I don't need the distraction."

The girls skulked out the door to the first window they could press their noses against and watched.

Cliff removed the towel from her head and placed a bowl of scalding water on the table. "I will be as tender as I can." He poured another drink into her cup and a small amount into one of her china bowls. He then placed both the thread and needle in the whiskey. "Are you ready?"

"Do your worst," Lavina slurred while Cliff poured whiskey on the wound. "For all that is holy. You might have warned me that was coming," Lavina yelled.

"Sorry, next I will shave the hair back."

"Glory be. I am going to look so ugly." She placed her face in her hands and whimpered. "Ted will not want me now."

Cliff smoothed her hair. "Then he is not worth your time. There are many men who would take you bald."

Lavina leaned her head against his chest. "You're so nice to me." She sniffed. "And dang, you smell good."

"It's your soap." Cliff chuckled and pushed her head forward. "Hold still or you will be bald."

"Can you sew up a person?"

"Yes, you'd be surprised what my mother had to learn. Once I was old enough to go to town by myself, she never left the ranch again."

Lavina turned to face him. "Why not?"

Cliff pushed her head back into position. "Well, funny enough, people are more accepting of a black bastard than his white mama who slept with a black man."

Lavina leaned against his chest once more. "Why are people so awful to one another?" Cliff nudged her forward as she said, "You realize they are going to be amazed to see who made it to heaven first."

"I imagine they will." He laid the razor on the table and threaded the needle.

Lavina giggled. "Can you picture it? Your mama at the pearly gates with Saint Peter. One of those self-righteous biddies tries to get in and she gets to say, 'They need to go to hell.' Can you see their faces?" She lapsed into a giggling fit.

Cliff shook his head and grinned. "Okay, drink more. This is going to hurt."

"I am trusting you, giant." Lavina filled her cup again and threw it back. "Down the hatch."

When Cliff had finished sewing his inebriated, gregarious patient, he called for the girls. "You girls go fetch Lavina's cot then start eggs and bacon. I need to keep a close eye on her tonight."

"Yes, Pa."

Lavina turned once they left and came eye to chest with Cliff. "Oh, my goodness. I hope Ted has a hairy chest." She wrapped a curl around her finger. "Every time I look at yours, I just want to bite it." She grabbed his chest and pretended to bite. "Rarrrr."

Cliff chuckled and took both her hands in his. "For your sake, I hope you don't remember tonight."

"Have you ever had pecan pie?"

"Not that I recall."

"It is this sugar and molasses and pecan sin-filled dessert. Every time I look at you, I think of it. Mmm. Someone get me a spoon. I could just eat you up."

"Sh," he whispered then moved away to help the girls through the door.

When he had her cot set up outside his bedroom door, he carried Lavina to it. "You just sit here. I will bring you a plate."

After everyone ate, he told the girls to head to bed. "It has been a long day."

Both girls ran to hug Lavina. "We are so sorry; we didn't mean to hurt you."

Lavina hugged them to her. "I am certain you did no such thing. This was my fault." She held them out and looked them in the eye. "I should have never tried to use that old wood in the first place. Now you go upstairs and dream of sweet things." She smiled at Cliff. "I am going to dream of eating me a big ole piece of pecan pie."

She closed her eyes as the girls shrugged their shoulders and giggled. Lavina snapped awake. "Prime example of why ladies do not drink whiskey. They get mouthy. Now y'all run along up to bed before my mouth gets away with me."

She kissed the girls, and Cliff watched as she swayed. "Are you going to be alright?" he asked. Lavina pursed her lips and shook her head. "Do you need to throw up?" She nodded as Cliff scooped her up and took her onto the porch, where she emptied her stomach.

"I am better now," she said, then wiped her mouth. "But I need to use the facilities." She stumbled toward the outhouse as Cliff caught her arm. "Awe, you are just the nicest guy. Poor Ted, he better be something else altogether." Lavina patted his hand. "Because you are some pretty stiff competition."

Cliff waited in the dark for her with a slight smile on his lips. *You need to tell her the truth.* When she exited, he put an arm around her waist to keep her from tripping and asked, "How upset might you be to find out someone deceived you?"

Lavina stopped and looked around the ranch. "I am not sure. I gained so much from coming here. There is a peace of mind in these mountains I never experienced in Georgia." She looked into his eyes. "I am not saying that prejudice doesn't exist here. It is just not a part of every conversation and in everything that happens."

Once they got to the porch, she turned and sat on the step. "I lived with an aunt who once said, 'I don't understand why they freed the blacks, they cannot find jobs now?' Forget that we sold off their wives and children to the highest bidder." She snorted. "She also said that before Lincoln came along, no one thought slavery was a bad thing. I guess she didn't read the part in the bible where Moses freed those slaves, because slavery, was a bad thing."

Cliff smiled and pulled her to her feet. "I will ask you again tomorrow when the whiskey has worn off."

"You asked me a question?"

Cliff chuckled. "Yes, but I'll wait until we both understand what the other is saying."

Lavina fell against his chest and wrapped her arms around his waist. "I was talking of poor Ted, never being able to live up to the lofty standards you set for me as to what a man should be." She gave his nipple a slight nibble.

"All right." He unwound her arms and scooped her off her feet. "It's time you got to sleep." He chuckled low as he walked her in and laid her on his bed. "I will sleep on your cot and leave the door open. Just call out if you need anything."

Lavina wrapped her arms around his neck and whispered against his lips. "Anything?"

"Anything within reason." He slid out of her grasp and blew out the light.

"Then you best get me a bucket." A loud belch came from deep within her throat. Cliff leaped over the cot, grabbed a pail, and put it under her head just in time. As she filled his milk bucket, he relit the lantern. "I'm not sure if it is the alcohol or the head injury, but I am not doing so good."

"I imagine a little of both." He left to get a bowl of cold water and a washcloth. "Here." He handed her the cool cloth and took the pail. "Put this on your head while I empty the bucket." As he walked out, fear swept over him. *I hope the alcohol is the cause.* He had heard of people who dropped over dead days after a head injury.

When he reentered the bedroom. Laid back against his pillow, Lavina held the cloth over her eyes. He placed the pail on the floor by her head and whispered, "It's right here if you need it during the night."

Lavina did not open her eyes as she said, "Thank you, Cliff. You need to go to sleep so you can work in the morning."

Cliff blew out the lantern once more. "I will send the girls to tell them I am staying home to keep an eye on you. If something happened to you tomorrow, neither the girls nor I could live with it."

"Plus, I'd be dead." She giggled.

"There's that too," he teased as he lay on her cot and inhaled her intoxicating aroma.

"To answer your question." She spoke in hushed tones, and Cliff rolled toward her voice in the darkened room.

"I could not leave Idaho now for any perceived deception. I found my place, my calling. I had no dreams for myself before I came here. But now

I know how I want to spend my life." She paused for what seemed to Cliff an eternity. "If a deception brought me here and taught me what I now know, I am glad of it. I am a better person for it." Another long, nerve-racking silence came from her.

Tell her it was you who deceived her. "Lavina." Cliff resigned himself to come clean. "I've wanted to tell you for a long while what having you here has meant to me and the girls. But we have done things we are not proud of in order to keep you here. I am sorry for the deception, but as you said, if it brought us to this moment..."

"Ronccc ronc pshshsh."

The sound of her snores caused Cliff to chuckle. "I guess we can talk another time."

"RONC ronc dishyoushay pshsh."

"Good night, Lavina... My love." His soft-spoken declaration died in the air between them and drifted to the floor as Lavina's drunken snores increased.

Chapter Twenty-One

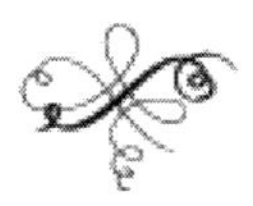

Milly descended the ladder first with a head full of anxiety and asked her father, "How did she do last night?"

"Lots of moaning." Cliff had made breakfast and sat the plates on the table. "I want you girls to run over to the Glascocks and tell them I need to stay here and keep an eye on Lavina today."

Milly looked toward the bedroom. "Is she that bad, Pa?"

"I just worry if she took a fall or did too much today, she might get worse." He drank a sip of coffee and announced, "The time has come to tell her the truth about Ted's letters."

Shock filled Milly's eyes. *I can't let him do that.* "No Pa, please. We love her." Milly elbowed Tilly.

"Yeah Pa, we don't want her to go."

Cliff shook his head. "We love her is why we are going to tell her the truth."

Milly's mind twisted and turned into a scramble for her next plot. "Can you please wait until we get back?"

"I think it's best if I do it alone and leave you girls out of it."

"No!" Milly glanced at the bedroom door and lowered her voice. "We need to be there to explain how we talked you into it."

"I assume she won't care why I did it."

Milly held his hand. "But Pa, we did the lying share, and we can take the blame." She nudged her sister again, who nodded in agreement. "Don't you see Pa? She can love Tilly and me to the moon and back and still leave. You are our only chance of her staying. If she understands that you got caught up in our plot, she might not get so upset and leave." She watched her father's face as he thought on her words. "Promise me you won't say a word until we get home."

Cliff took a deep breath and let it out with a sigh. "Fine, but it happens today."

Milly stuck out her pinky. "Promise me."

He linked pinkies and shook on it. "Promise."

Once they were out of view of the house, Milly released a tirade. "We cannot let this happen. We must prevent Pa from telling her. She will pack up so fast it will make your head spin."

Tilly sucked her hair. "How can we prevent it?"

Milly stopped and put both hands on her sister's shoulders. "We must think hard. Like we never thought before."

They remained each in their own thoughts for the rest of the trip to the Glascocks. Rocky and Randy were stepping out of the door as the girls approached. "Miss Lavina is not doing so well. Pa stayed home with her."

Randy patted Tilly's downcast head. "Don't be so sad, I am sure she will be fine." Tilly burst into tears and ran inside to throw herself on Missus Glascock's lap.

Milly gave the boys a nervous grin. "I am sure you're right and Pa will be back at work in the morning."

Both men rubbed her head. "Go on in," Rocky said. "Ma has cookies."

Milly walked in to see Tilly spilling the whole of their story to Missus Glascock. The old lady looked up and snapped. "Well, you can't let him tell her the truth."

"There is nothing we can do now. He is determined," Milly said as she sat in the chair across from the wiry old woman.

"Then you must make it impossible for him to tell her."

Milly snorted. "How can we do that? She's got ears, and he is going to be talking."

"Ain't no man going to give that kind of news to a dying woman."

"Dying?" Tilly screamed from her perch on Missus Glascock's knee.

"Well, not dying, but close enough. Now stand and let me rise." She stood and walked to a cupboard. "You say he will not tell her until you get home?"

"That's right he promised."

"I need you girls to go out and weed my garden today. That way you won't be home until dark when you can carry out my plan."

"What plan?"

"I will tell you before you leave so as you don't forget. Scoot now, to the garden. I will cook a special treat for your new Ma."

The girls both giggled and hugged the wise old Irish woman, then ran into the garden. They spent the entire day weeding, except for lunch, which they ate at the table with the grin-ridden Missus Glascock. As they prepared to leave, the old lady held a small vile out to Milly. "Now this bottle is syrup of ipecac. It induces vomiting. It only takes a drop or two in her food and she will get sick."

Milly reached out a shaky hand and took the vile. "It won't hurt her?"

"No, you can give that to babies when they eat something they shouldn't." She patted the girls' heads. "Give it to her as soon as you get home. I am sending you home with fresh soda bread. You tell her it's good Irish bread. Put a drop of ipecac on the butter. She will not taste it." She stood and pulled a mason jar from the cupboard. "I brewed her tea. It has laudanum in it which will make her drowsy. You tell her it will ease her stomach." She poured the tea into the jar and sealed the lid.

Tilly had half her hair sucked into her mouth while Milly smiled at Missus Glasscock as she led them onto the porch. "You tell your pa, that he needs to bring his wagon over first thing in the morning. Tell him they are taking the first load of ore to the train station and that with his wagon it will save days of hauling." She kissed the girls' heads. "He won't be back until the next afternoon. Perchance my boys will have convinced him how foolish it will be to tell her of the deception. They may even convince him to marry Lavina and stop this foolishness with Ted Bartlett."

As the girls walked home, Milly worried for Tilly, who acted sullen since yesterday. "I will do everything. You don't need to get upset. It will work and Lavina will be fine."

Tilly pulled the hair from her mouth. "I am not upset with the plan. Yesterday when I stayed with Lavina, she took forever to wake up. I thought she was dead." Tears flowed over her cheeks. "Now, Pa wants her to leave. It's as if God doesn't want us to have a Ma."

Milly held her sister's hand. "I understand. That is why I intend to do anything to keep her."

The girls leaned into each other. "We have been good girls. Why can't we have a Ma without being sneaky?" Tilly continued to cry.

"I don't know, but I am tired of not having one. I love Pa, but he cannot teach us to be ladies as good as Lavina can. She is ours, we earned her, and Ted is going to have to find another."

The girls walked home with a new determination.

"Did you see the team of horses and stagecoach that ran me over?" Lavina asked as she aimed straight for the coffee pot.

Cliff chuckled. "No, but I saw a fifth of whiskey, both coming and going."

Lavina sat at the table. "Ow, don't make me laugh." She held her head and touched her blood-matted hair. "I need a bath."

Cliff handed her a plate of eggs and examined her stitches. "They don't appear infected and are holding nicely."

As her fingers caressed the wound, she felt the stubble of her shaved hair. "How ridiculous do I look?"

"You look to be a very lucky woman." He bent and kissed her head.

A blush burned her cheeks as she searched her memory. "I have an uneasy impression I owe you an apology."

Cliff sat with his coffee and asked, "Concerning what?"

"Hum?" Lavina smiled. "I am uncertain. Last night is a blur of emotions and memories." She ate her eggs. *Did I bite his nipple? Oh, glory be. I could not have been that drunk.*

Cliff gave her a slight grin. "No harm, no foul. We have both forgotten last night."

The sense he was lying, and she had indeed made a fool of herself, was overpowering. "Where are the girls?" she asked then glanced around the house.

"I sent them to tell Rocky and Randy I could not come to work today. I imagine Missus Glascock is taking advantage of the girls, by having them weed her garden. She had mentioned it might be nice if they could come over and do just that."

Lavina rubbed her temples. "Dear, my head is swimming, and my hair is nasty." She pulled a strand of blood-soaked hair out. "Do you mind if I bathed and leave the dishes for later?"

Cliff snorted. "Lavina, you don't need to always be cleaning up after us. I got this." He gathered her plate and cup. "Go take a bath. Leave both doors open a bit. In case you need to call out for help."

"Thank you, I will." She stood and walked with caution to the shed as she fought back a dizzy spell. *I so thought I might wake up and be back to normal. It must be a mixture of alcohol and accident.*

Lavina had been in the bath for over an hour when Cliff called to her. "Are you alive in there?"

"Yes, I am enjoying it so much that I keep adding more hot water."

He headed out to finish the clothesline. It took an hour to make a tight stable line, yet Lavina still did not exit the bathhouse. Inside the cabin, he stripped his bedding and washed it in the sink, then hung it on the new line. *Lavina can stay in my bed until she feels well enough to move back into the shed.*

As he headed back to the house, Lavina stepped out at last. "It took a while to get the soap and blood out. I didn't want to dunk my head in the water for fear that the sulfur might infect it," she said as they walked into the house together.

Cliff pulled out a chair and took her brush from her hand. "I will put honey and cheesecloth on the wound today," he said as he brushed the knots from her hair.

"Thank you."

He then cut the cheesecloth and dabbed on honey. He pulled the hair from the front of the scar and weaved it into the hair behind her wound. "As long as you don't get too wild, that should keep it in place."

Lavina held her mirror up to inspect it. "I can't even see the cut. I don't know what to say, you're a genuine artist."

Cliff held both sides of her head and placed a soft kiss on her hair. "I want you to remember no matter what happens, the girls and I appreciate everything you have done for us. And remember that we have done what we have done because of our affection for you." Cliff walked to the counter and cut the leftover roast. *Father in heaven, please don't let her hate us for deceiving her.*

Lavina frowned at his back. "I heard your words but failed to understand their meaning. My mind is swimming in mud." Cliff handed her a plate without alleviating her thoughts, but she refused his offer. "I could not eat just now. I think I will lie down for a while." She moved to her cot and turned her back on him.

The moment the girls walk through the door, I am telling her the truth. I will not let them talk me out of it again.

The chances of her leaving them, Cliff was certain, were low. *If she is not a woman in love, then I don't know what one looks like.* He knew she might pack and leave at first, but he intended to use everything in his arsenal to assure her return. *People cannot turn love off. She loves us, and she will see in time that we did what we did, out of our love for her.*

He sauntered out to the line and gathered his bedding. After he made his bed, he climbed the ladder to the girls' room and pulled theirs as well. He then washed and hung them, chopped wood, and started dinner. The entire time he worked, Lavina never stirred.

Dusk was setting in, and he began to worry why the girls were so late. *Tilly will be half frightened out of her skin by every sound.* Tilly was safe in the house every night before dark since the bear incident. He often wished Tilly was more like Milly, and vice versa. *Perhaps that is the way with twins. They each have weaknesses to draw on each other's strengths.*

No, Cliff would not change his girls for the world, but he hoped to change the world for his girls. *They will be angry at me for a time, but they will soon see why it was important to tell Lavina the truth.* He gathered their sheets from the line and discerned their chatter from a distance. With a furrowed brow, he walked into the house and found Lavina sitting at the table.

"Dinner smells wonderful. I am starving."

Cliff ladled her up the elk stew he made. "Sorry, no bread or biscuits, but I am not half the chef you are." He heard the girls on the porch. *The moment of truth.* Cliff ladled out three more bowls and prepared himself to tell the entire story to Lavina.

CHAPTER TWENTY-TWO

When Milly stepped into the house, she took a deep breath. "Oh my, it smells delicious in here."

"Your daddy made stew."

Tilly pushed past her sister. "We brought Irish biscuits, and a tea Missus Glascock said might help settle your stomach."

"How grand, I would love a biscuit." Lavina rubbed her hands together. "I am famished."

Milly placed them on the counter and buttered one as Tilly blocked her from view by pouring the jar of tea into the teapot on the table. The biscuits were triangular, and Milly placed two drops of ipecac from her pocket on the tip of one end. She took care to hand it to Lavina so that the tip would be the last bite.

Once Tilly set the teapot on the stove to heat, the girls sat, and Cliff led them in the blessing. Milly worried she might be the only one to chatter on to prevent their father from having his conversation before Lavina got sick. However, Tilly spoke first. "I am so glad you are better, Miss Lavina." She smiled at her father and said with pride in her voice, "Oh Pa, it was so frightening yesterday. But you would have been proud of me. I kept the cloth tight on her head and didn't fall to pieces as I wanted to."

Cliff mussed her hair. "I am proud of you, baby girl."

"I was brave even when I heard a noise behind the house, and I thought it was a bear coming because it could smell the blood. I just screamed loud and woke Miss Lavina. There were no more sounds after that. I either scared off the animal or it was never a bear and Miss Lavina being awake scared off my imaginations."

Milly never admired her sister as she did tonight. She watched with anticipation as Lavina came to the last bite of bread and kicked Tilly under the table. The girls both held their breath as she popped it into her mouth.

Lavina chewed twice, and with no warning, heaved the contents of her guts onto the table. The girls sat in shock as it first splashed on the table's surface, then ricocheted in their faces. They managed to push their chairs away from the table before they both vomited into their laps. Cliff was the only one fortunate enough to make it to the porch before revisiting his dinner.

When he reentered, the three women in his life were crying and apologizing to one another.

"I am sorry, that came out of nowhere," Lavina explained.

"I am sorry, I didn't think it could happen like that." Tilly smacked Milly on the back of the head to stop her from speaking. Milly then froze as she misread the scowl on Cliff's face.

"We will clean it up, Pa."

He took their towels from the drying hook by the stove and handed them to the girls. "No, you two go bathe and wash your clothes after you're through. Lavina, sit in the rocker, I will bring you a cup of Missus Glascock's brew."

He pulled a clean cup from the shelf because Lavina's tea service now needed a thorough washing. He handed her the cup, then cut two small pieces of cheesecloth and stuffed it in his nose. "I will clean this up myself."

Milly and Tilly giggled as they grabbed a lantern and headed for the bathhouse.

Once Cliff had the dishes in the sink, he folded the tablecloth in on itself and placed it on the counter. *Well, that saved a lot of cleanup.* He used one of Lavina's spatulas and a bowl to scrape the carnage off the floor, then got on his knees and scrubbed. He then stood and emptied both containers into the yard. As he reentered, he saw Lavina flopped on her cot, sound asleep.

One down, two to go.

It was then he remembered the girls' blankets were still on the line. He grabbed a lantern and headed back to his clothesline. With the dry blankets in hand, he climbed the ladder up to the loft and made the bed. "Put your clothes on the counter," he told them when they entered. "I will hang them up after I wash the tablecloth."

Milly walked to stand over Lavina. "She fell asleep that fast?" she asked. "Do you suppose she is going to be alright?"

As Milly placed her foot on the bottom step of the ladder, Cliff mussed her hair with his giant paw. "We will have to wait and see how she is in the morning."

Tilly pulled on his sleeve. "We forgot to tell you. Missus Glascock said for you to bring the wagon in the morning. They are taking the first load of ore to the train station."

"She said with three wagons running, it will save a trip or two," Milly added.

Cliff's brow furrowed as he walked to the sink and turned on the faucet. "Can you girls handle things here by yourselves?"

The girls rushed to his side. "Yes, Pa," Tilly spoke first. "If something bad happens, one of us will run to town for help. The other one will stay with Miss Lavina."

"We won't let bad things happen though." Milly interrupted. "We will make sure Miss Lavina doesn't need to do anything while you're away."

He pulled the girls to him and kissed their heads. "That's my girls. I knew I could count on you. Now you need to get to bed." The girls kissed his cheek and headed for the loft. "Hold up a minute." He walked to where they were and knelt in front of them. "I don't want any shenanigans tomorrow. The deception stops tonight." Both girls bent their heads. "Do you understand me?" He lifted their chins. "That means no plots or plans or trumped-up games." He shook Milly's chin. "Milly Sly, are you listening? I need you to be good."

"Yes, Pa. I hear you," she said.

Tilly snuggled into Cliff's chest. "I will be good, Pa."

Cliff mussed her hair. "I know you will, my Tilly girl. I was making certain your sister got her silly notions out of her head."

Tilly winked at Milly, who stuck out her tongue and said, "I heard you. No more silly ideas."

After the girls went to bed, their whispers filtered down the stairs the entire time Cliff washed dishes and linens. Once he finished hanging them on the line, silence came from the loft.

He scrubbed the counters and table one last time and looked around the room. Lavina flopped on her back and snorted. Cliff removed her slippers and covered her with a blanket then knelt at her head and kissed her brow. "Good night, my love," he whispered against her flesh. Giggles came from the loft. "Good night, girls," he barked.

"Good night, Pa." They giggled again.

The thirty minutes Tilly had spent as she waited for Lavina to wake up were the longest in her young life. The effect the stress took on her changed her in ways that surprised even herself.

I will be a strong, confident woman and I will let no one or anything frighten me or make me feel as if I am not good enough. When they climbed the ladder, she was the first to speak. "Did you understand what he said?"

"Yes. I don't intend to lie to her anymore, I plan to tell her many truths."

"No, I meant about you being Milly Sly. It didn't even cross his mind that I was being sneaky and preventing him from talking to Lavina tonight."

Milly climbed into bed. "Of course not. Why would he?"

"Don't you see? If he didn't notice, neither will Lavina. We can use this to our advantage tomorrow." She held her sister's hands as she knelt facing her on the bed. "And I have a very sneaky idea. No lying, no deception as you said, just truths."

Milly flipped back the cover. "Slip in and talk softly so Pa won't hear."

"Tomorrow you talk Pa up to Lavina, in the same way, you did for her to Pa. She will think you are up to something and will come to talk with me to get away from the foolishness of it."

Milly furrowed her brow. "How will that help?"

"She will assume everything I say is not a plot to trap her. So, I will say things such as, 'It was nice to see Pa having fun fishing, that is the first real fun he has had since grandma died. He is so stressed out trying to do everything by himself.'"

"Oh, that's good. I did not think you had this in you. I like it."

Tilly smiled at her sister and took the lead. "Now listen, you need to set up opportunities for me."

"Such as what?"

"You say something about how you might like to get a love letter. I will say, remember how Pa just started to teach us our letters when grandma took sick."

"Gosh Tilly, you have clever ideas." Admiration filled her sister's voice.

Tilly flopped back on her pillow, self-satisfied. "We are going to be two of the most pathetic orphans she ever met." Milly squeezed her hand. "But remember, all the while you have to be talking Pa up, to distract her from realizing I am the one plotting and planning."

"Tilly?" a sullen tone filled Milly's voice. "Do you ever wonder how other sisters think?"

Tilly rolled toward her. "What do you mean?"

"I mean normal sisters, not twins." She snuggled closer to Tilly.

"Sometimes. Like when we understand what the other is thinking by a glance. Or how I can sense when you are sad or happy, even when I can't see you."

"Yeah, like that. Or when we know that the only other person on earth who understands us, is the other. I am never lonely because I know you are here. Even when grandma died..."

"I thought at least Milly would always be here for me." Tilly finished her sentence.

Milly threw her arms around her twin's neck. "Exactly."

"Why are you bringing this up now?" Tilly asked as she leaned on her elbow.

"I want you to know that no matter what happens. Whether Lavina stays or leaves, I will always love you first before all others."

Tilly laid her head beside her sister. "And I will always love you, before all others."

"Do you suppose that will change when we get married?" Doubt now crept into their minds.

"Well, we can do what Lavina did and advertise in one of those magazines that we are twins in search of twins to marry. That way our husbands might understand just how we feel and not be mad."

It was Milly's turn to lean on her elbow. "Geeze Tilly you need to slow up on the plotting and planning or I won't have anything that makes me unique."

Tilly laughed. "You should start chewing your hair, then no one could tell us apart." That was the moment their father reentered the house, and they fell silent.

Both girls crawled up and glanced over the rail to see him kiss Lavina. Their giggles made him snap, "Good night, girls."

"Good night, Pa." They said in unison and giggled again as they locked hands and slid back into bed.

"We are going to make Lavina his," Milly said as she turned her back on her sister.

"Yes, we are." Tilly scooched against her twin's warm back. "And bury her silly dreams of Ted in the backyard."

CHAPTER TWENTY-THREE

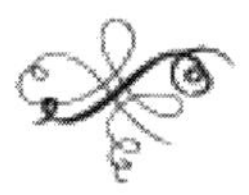

Tilly and Milly moved Lavina's cot back into her shed and set out her paints. She painted her naked ladies while they fashioned makeshift clothes from Lavina's sheer material. Tilly let Milly talk throughout the morning about the attributes of their father. Lavina rolled her eyes while Milly gave silent prods for Tilly to speak.

The time is not right. Tilly waited with patients until it was. At last, she cut her eyes in the door's direction. Milly laid aside her scissors and stood. "It is time I started lunch." She winked at Tilly and exited.

"Well, my, my. This has been an enlightening morning. I was sure your sister might never run out of the marvelous deeds of Cliff Walker." Lavina laced her voice with snark as she continued to paint.

Tilly pounced on the opportunity provided to her. "Pay no never mind to her Miss Lavina, she is just worried for Pa."

"Worried." Lavina turned to face her.

"Yeah, about how he will react when you leave us." Tilly kept her eyes on her work. "You see, grandma said when our Ma died, Pa didn't eat for three weeks straight."

"Oh, dear." Tilly recognized the shock in Lavina's voice and continued with her tale of woe.

"She said he sat around and moaned and did his work like a machine, with no care or passion." She cut another piece of fabric. "Grandma took care of us while he walked around a shell of a man, she said." Tilly held the fabric in front of her face and pretended to examine it with care. "Grandma decided she could not let it go on any longer and devised a plan." Tilly stood and draped the cloth over one of the fresh paintings. "What do you think of this?"

"Fine, fine." Lavina fanned the air. "Go on with your story. What was her plan?"

"One night Pa came in from working and sat in his chair. Grandma had a bag packed, waiting by the door. She picked up Milly and me, then placed us on his lap." Tilly acted it out for her audience of one. "She then grabbed her bag and told him she was going to visit a friend for a few days."

"Oh, goodness."

"It worked. When Grandma came home, he was back to eating. We were healthy and happy, and so was Pa."

Lavina's chin quivered as she whispered. "Your grandmother was a wise woman."

Tilly sat on the floor once more. "She sure was, and when she died, again Pa stopped eating and walked around an empty shell. So, one day when he came in from the field, Milly and I curled up in his lap to help him mourn. He rocked us until we fell asleep. The next morning when we crawled off his lap he said, 'I could eat a horse. What do my baby girls want for breakfast?' And all was well."

Tilly still avoided eye contact but heard Lavina as she sniffled and wiped away tears.

With child-like carelessness, Tilly stood and flounced to the door. "So, you see, I realize Pa will be unhappy for a few weeks and not eat again when you leave. But he has his girls to bring him out of it." She stepped into the sunlight to look up at the sky, then put a fake forlorn tone in her voice, "I just don't know who will get Milly and me through it." She waited for the inevitable moan to escape Lavina's lips, then skipped toward the cabin. "I am going to get us a blanket to sit on, so we can have a picnic lunch in the sun."

As she entered the house, Tilly clapped. "Oh, Milly, you should have been there. That was a performance of a lifetime."

Milly made sandwiches and placed them on the tray. "Do you suppose our plan is working?"

Tilly pulled a blanket from her father's bed and ran back to the kitchen. "She is in the shed bawling like a baby. Let's give her a minute to pull herself together before we set up our picnic."

The girls peeked out the window and watched as Lavina wiped away her tears and straightened her dress before Tilly spoke again. "Listen, during lunch, don't even mention Pa. Let's just talk about the paintings and how we are going to dress them. When we go back to work, only say a few nice things about Pa. When you go to make dinner, I will give her another heart-breaking story. After we clean up dinner, we will go to bed and let her worry over us poor orphans and the gentle giant that needs a wife."

They set up their lunch with giggles and carefree chatter. They talked of the day and how the summer was near completion. How they wanted to find a good deep swimming hole and make a rope swing. They talked on many subjects but never mentioned their father until back in the shed after they cleaned up lunch.

As she walked in, Milly winked at Tilly. "Our Pa is a wonderful singer?"

Lavina glanced at Tilly, who rolled her eyes and mouthed, '*We will be fine.'*

"I had no idea," Lavina said.

"Grandma always said he should be on stage." She picked up a piece of pre-cut fabric and held it against the wall. "How are we going to get the cloth to stay?"

Lavina set her palate and brush on the stack of wood and said, "I have packed this old trunk around for years, as I moved from family to family. It has seen better days. So, I have a repair kit to tack it back together when necessary." She pulled out a box of half-inch trunk tacks and a small hammer. "These will do just fine."

Milly snatched them up and moved to start on her first toga, while Tilly motioned for her silence. "Why did you move so much?" Tilly asked.

"No one wanted to bother with the raising of me. Too headstrong, I guess."

"Our grandma had to work hard. Right alongside Pa. That is not the same as you, but it would have been nice to eat something other than stew or beans."

Lavina turned and furrowed her brow. "That's all you ate."

Tilly signaled Milly to corroborate her story. "Yeah, at night grandma put on a pot of stew or beans, and the next day we ate it for every meal."

Tilly pulled up her sleeve. "Until we got big enough to cook eggs and bacon for ourselves." She showed Lavina a mangled burn mark. "I did this the second time we made breakfast." She pulled up her elbow to examine the scar. "It wouldn't have healed so bad, but we hid it from Pa and Grandma so we could keep cooking."

Milly laughed. "Yeah, because we couldn't get the smell of beans out of our bed." Both girls giggled and accused the other of the retched smells that emanated from their bedding.

Lavina knelt and held Tilly's arm. "You pitiful thing. What did you do for it? This looks as if it hurt something terrible."

"Well, it happened right before Grandma walked in, so I leaned against the wall until she left. When I pulled away, my skin stayed on the wall."

Lavina grimaced and hugged Tilly to her as the girls winked at each other. Milly jumped in to finish the tragic tale of two sisters. "I tried my best to help. I put honey and cheesecloth and wrapped it up every day until it healed."

Lavina's mouth dropped open. "And no one noticed?"

"Life was hard on the farm. Work needed doing and there was little time for fussing." Tilly made her voice sound as matter-of-fact as possible. "Sides, it's what you got to do with no Ma. You understand, don't you? Because you didn't have a ma or a pa."

Milly chimed in, "As Grandma used to say, you just do your best and pray for the rest."

Lavina hugged the girls to her breast. "True, life is hard with no mother to care for you." The girls gave each other the thumbs-up behind Lavina's back. She stood and dusted her knees, and the girls saw compassion and sympathy in her eyes as her chin quivered. "But a strong woman can make her trials into triumphs. Come, ladies, let's concentrate on happier things." She retrieved her palette and made a few brush strokes. "So, what songs does your daddy sing."

A looked past between the girls and the most wicked smiles crossed their lips as they began to sing.

Rescue the perishing, care for the dying,
snatch them in pity from sin and the grave.
weep o'er the erring one, lift up the fallen,
tell them of Jesus the mighty to save.

Lavina stared at them as her jaw dropped. Tilly pulled Milly close as they belted out the chorus.

Rescue the perishing,
care for the dying.
Jesus is merciful,
Jesus will save.

They began to act out the words as they sang.

Though they are slighting Him, still He is waiting,

waiting the penitent child to receive.

They fell to their knees in front of her with their hands folded in prayer.

plead with them earnestly, plead with them gently,

He will forgive if they only believe.

They stood and waved their hands in the air as they sang the chorus again. They then circled their arms around Lavina and swayed back and forth as they continued.

Down in the human heart, crushed by the tempter,

feelings lie buried that grace can restore.

touched by a loving heart, wakened by kindness,

chords that are broken will vibrate once more.

They grabbed her hands and watched her fight back tears as they marched to the music.

Rescue the perishing, duty demands it.

Strength for thy labor the Lord will provide.

back to the narrow way patiently win them,

tell the poor wanderer a Savior has died.

As they sang the chorus one last time Lavina swallowed hard and held her hand in front of her gaping mouth. The look in her eyes was pure horror.

"What's wrong, Miss Lavina?" Tilly added extra innocence to her question.

Lavina balled her fist and pressed a knuckle against her lips. "Ah... I will go inside the cabin and start dinner," she said in slow choppy syllables.

Both girls shrugged. "That's fine, we will finish this toga and be right behind you."

As Lavina headed toward the house, the girls sang, *touched by a loving heart, wakened by kindness,* then smiled in triumph as Lavina ran inside and slammed the door.

CHAPTER TWENTY-FOUR

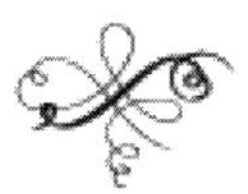

Lavina was never so happy to see the girls go to bed. *Glory be, what am I to do now?* The entire day, memories of her time here cluttered her mind. Her talk with Cliff when he told her, that dreams do not always fulfilled in the way you expect them to. You need to be open to them becoming something new. Missus Glascock's advice of how she should not throw away a good man in search of the dream of a better one. Visions of herself playing a mother bear as she stared down a real bear. Not to mention her excitement at Cliff's every touch that coursed through her veins.

Today every feminine fiber in her body wished nothing more than to touch them with a loving heart and waken them to kindness. *How am I ever going to think Ted is enough after today?* Her head swam with doubt and guilt as she crawled into Cliff's bed.

The next morning, she made pancakes for the girls and enjoyed their giggles and gratitude while she drank her coffee. "I was thinking we should stroll into town today and see if they have any pecans. I've had a powerful craving for pecan pie the last couple of days."

The girls squealed and scampered up the ladder. "Should we wear our best dress, Miss Lavina?" Milly asked.

"Yes ma'am. We will hit the town in grand style." Lavina walked to the shed, put on her most elaborate dress, and found a small hat. Light enough not to put pressure on her wound, but big enough to cover it. She found two Bebe hats for the girls, which had tiny curtains at the back, and a high coronet in front.

"We are high-stepping it now, ladies," Lavina said as she let them peer into her hand mirror.

As they passed the pond, Tilly asked, "Where are the geese?"

Lavina sighed. "I imagine they flew south for the winter. The days are growing shorter, and the nights are getting cooler."

"Do you suppose they flew to Georgia?"

Lavina shivered. "Somebody just walked over my grave."

Milly cut her eyes at her. "What does that mean?"

"I am not sure, just an omen of something not right with the world." Lavina brushed off the prophetic sense that she had come with the geese and now must leave with them.

The gentlemen in the store made quite the fuss over the girls. "Prettiest gals I've ever seen," Davis teased.

Carl smiled and told them, "You just missed your Pa and the Glasscock boys."

Lavina leaned on the counter. "Oh, nice. They are back early girls. Your Pa might be home for lunch."

"Did not sound that way," Davis said as he folded his paper. "They said they were going to load the wagons tonight, so they could head out at first light and make the trip in one day instead of two."

"That will give us time to bake that pecan pie before he gets home,"

Lavina said to the girls, then smiled at Carl. "That is if you have pecans and sweet molasses," she said in her simpering southern belle drawl.

Carl blushed. "As a matter of fact Miss Lavina, I have both." He pulled a jar of molasses from the shelf behind him, then heaved a twenty-five-pound bag of pecans onto the counter. "How many pounds do you need?"

"Oh, I am sure two will be plenty." She batted her eyes, and the girls giggled. "You two come here and pick out one hard candy each."

The bell on the front door jingled as she handed Carl the money. All eyes turned to see a short, plump, pockmarked peacock. Dressed in the height of fashion. "Good afternoon, I just arrived from Savana, Georgia," she said down her enormous nose. "Ted Bartlett, my fiancé, sent me ahead to hire someone to repair Mac Tilman's old mining shack."

All eyes turned to Lavina as the floor melted under her feet and a wave of heat washed over her. She felt her corset shrink around her ribs and cut off her breath.

"Ted said there was a high-yellow nigger by the name of Cliff, that might be available to do the work."

If this twit could have said one thing to put the fight back into Lavina, it was the term she just used.

Tilly pulled on Lavina's sleeve. "Miss, is she talking about our Pa?"

Lavina bent and gave the girls her *'I'm going to skin this snake,'* look and said, "You ladies head on home now. I will catch up with y'all later."

The twins slinked past the newcomer, hand in hand, while Lavina straightened her skirt.

"Do you know Cliff? Where those his children?" The woman stared after the girls.

"Yes." The tone in Lavina's voice was warning enough to make Carl and Davis take a step backward. "I am Mister Walker's housekeeper and his girls' nanny."

The woman placed a chubby hand on her ample breast and rolled her eyes in disgust. "Oh, my. You're a nanny to two little pickaninnies." She then cackled. "Bless your heart, the mere idea must horrify your family."

Lavina drew herself up to her full height. "I am Ex-Governor Rufus Bullock's niece."

The stranger rolled her eyes again. "Well, that explains everything."

"Does it?" Lavina's voice was a cavalry charge, this ignorant pimple-faced heifer did not heed. "Let me educate you on another matter." Lavina ran her eyes in a slow upward assessment of her prey. "My dear, you are number eight in the long line of disillusioned fiancés of one, Theodore Bartlett." She watched the woman's plump jaw drop. "If I were you, I would keep a tight hold on my purse strings. You see, Ted sank one or more of those lady's fortunes into his played-out hole in the ground." Lavina then gave an ominous glare to Carl and Davis. "Isn't that right, gentlemen?"

"Yes, ma'am," they snapped out with fear-thickened voices.

Her eyes narrowed as she turned from the two cowards. "The poor dears had to scurry home with nothing but dirt in their pockets and pretty promises in their ears."

The woman clutched her purse with both hands and jerked it to her chin.

"Now if y'all will excuse me. I need to hurry on home and get the *master of the house's* dinner on the stove." Lavina turned to Carl, who thrust out her sack of supplies and gave an awkward show of his teeth. As Lavina stepped onto the stoop, she heard the frightened voice of the newcomer inquire as to the arrival of the next stage heading east.

Lavina walked down the dusty road with her head held high and a smile on her lips. *I may have enjoyed that a little too much.* She could have felt sympathy for the pudgy wench had she not been such an ignorant one. *After all, we are both in the same place now. Good riddance Ted Bartlett.*

As she walked past the empty pond, her heart felt free. *Sorry, my fare feathered friends; it looks as if I will not be heading south with you. I am home.*

She pulled Ted's letters from her satchel and tore them into. A small scrap of paper floated to the ground, and she bent to pick it up. It was the note Cliff wrote, to inform her that first week, that he left to look for work. As she read his bold handwriting, heat rose from her toes and did not stop until it reached her tongue, where it erupted. "That son of the south." She screamed. "I will kill him!"

As she approached the house, the girls ran out to greet her. Their faces told of their distress while Lavina fanned them away in irritation. "Girls, fix yourself lunch. I am not feeling like company just now. I will go lay on my bed for a while."

"We started potato soup for dinner," Milly said.

"Fine, girls, that's just fine. I will see you after a while." She sidestepped them, walked into her shed, and slammed the door.

"Have a nice nap, Miss Lavina," Tilly said as her chin quivered. "We hope you feel better soon."

Lavina sat and let her anger stew until it had scorched into a stinking mixture of revenge. *If he thinks for one moment, I will let him use me like this. He is sorely mistaken.* She flung open the door and stormed into the house to snatch up the milk bucket while the girls stepped back in fear. "Wash your socks! I'll wash your socks." She walked to the drain behind the bathhouse and scooped up the green slime that accumulated atop the copper-covered sulfur mulch. She stomped back past the girls into Cliff's room and slammed the door. "Clean your house, haul your wood, milk your cow." She yelled as she poured the goo on his bed and threw his clothes on top to smear it in deep.

Tilly and Milly banged on the door. "Miss Lavina, are you alright?"

Lavina snatched the door open. "Am I alright?" She bit off every word. "I am just fine and dandy, ladies. My head no longer swims, and my heart no longer aches."

"That's nice," Tilly said.

"Oh, one might think so, wouldn't they?"

Tilly opened her mouth to answer when Milly jerked her backward out of the house. "Shush dummy."

Cliff's voice greeted them from ten yards away. "Well, this is nice. My reasons for living have come out to welcome me home." The girls ran to him, and Lavina watched as Milly whispered in his ear.

Run along and give him the heads-up Milly Sly. Lavina walked into her shed and collected the letters as the Walkers entered their home. She took a deep breath and followed them.

Cliff sat relaxed at the table while the girls ladled soup into bowls with shaky hands. "Is there something wrong, Miss Lavina?" He asked with caution.

"Wrong?" Lavina hissed. "Why would you assume something was wrong?"

Cliff chuckled. "For one, by the way, you just asked that, and two, the girls assumed something had upset you in town today."

Lavina's entire body shook. "In town?" She tossed the letters in his face. "In town! You wrote me those letters, not Ted." Cliff sat up straight and opened his mouth to speak. "Shut up!" she screamed at the top of her lungs. "I have to ask myself why you would do this?" Tilly and Milly ran forward and started to speak on his behalf. "Shut up! No one needs to explain to me." She snapped in the girls' faces. "I know why." Lavina then turned back to Cliff. "You did this so I would clean your house, cook your meals, and wash your stinking socks!"

"No, no. That is not why," the girls screamed in unison as Cliff bowed his head and studied his folded hands.

"Please don't be mad at Pa." Tilly pleaded.

"Yeah, it was not his idea." Milly tugged at her sleeve.

"I am done. Done with y'all," she said as she walked toward the door. "You can keep my things, girls. I am packing a small bag and going to town to wait for the next stage with Ted's latest fiancé."

Tilly and Milly screamed as they ran and pinned her arms to her sides in a bear hug. "No, no. You can't go." Tears flowed from both their eyes.

Tilly suddenly snapped and yelled at Cliff, "Pa, you got to tell her the truth." But her father did not move from his chair.

Milly squeezed Lavina harder as she struggled to free herself. "We made Pa write the letters."

"Pa!" Tilly's voice filled with panic. "Tell her. Please tell her the truth."

Cliff stood at last and took a deep breath, then closed the gap between them. He searched Lavina's eyes and asked in a calm voice, "Truth. Do you want to hear the truth, Lavina?"

She tried to free herself, but the girls held on tighter. "That would be a refreshing change."

"The truth, then." He pressed up against her. "The truth is, I love you, Lavina." He smiled his deep dimpled smile, "I have loved you since the moment you kicked in my door and threw me out of my bed."

"Tell her she is pretty, Pa," Milly nudged.

"No." Tilly shook her head. "Ask her to marry us."

Cliff pushed Lavina's hair behind her ear as he breathed against it. "You are a beauty to behold. That is true." He then brushed his thumb across her lower lip and continued, "But more than that, you are the best thing to come into our lives. As Tilly says, you make us whole." He lifted her chin and placed a soft kiss on her upturned nose. "Will you marry us? And make us happy? Make us whole happy."

Lavina's entire body flushed with heat as she twisted in the girls' arms and snapped, "Let me go!"

Her words sliced through the air, and the pain of it showed on Cliff's face. He took a step back and tugged at the girl's sleeves. In a voice thick with defeat he said, "Let her go, girls. Lavina did not come here for us and we cannot hold her here any longer."

Milly and Tilly screamed *'FINE'* as they released their hold. Their angry little faces glared at their father, then turned down in a pout.

Lavina patted down her dress while she suppressed the emotions that threatened to cascade out and wash them all away. She pulled the downcast girls' chins up and said, "Ladies, I think you owe me an apology for your behavior tonight." Her reprimand did nothing to conceal the love she had for them.

Milly and Tilly, however, missed the tenderness in her eyes and jerked their chins from her grasp. "Sorry... Miss Lavina." They said in voices laced with snark.

Lavina pushed back on their foreheads as her eyes narrowed into slits. "That was all sass and no sorry." She then put her hands on her hips and tapped her foot on the floor. "What I think you meant to say, ladies, is, we truly apologize for our behavior, Ma."

Before she could take another breath, Cliff swept Lavina off her feet and kissed her with all the pent-up passions of a fur trapper after a long winter in the Rockies. The girls squealed, then held hands and danced around them singing, "Ring around the rosy, Pa grew a posey."

Lavina, for her part, was at long last able to devour his lips as if they were a slice of pecan pie. Fresh and hot right out of the oven.

Glory be Miss Walker, you sure can cook! Someone get me a spoon.

Made in United States
Cleveland, OH
16 January 2025

13467965R00105